By the same author
FIGHTING FIVE
WONDER BOY

Junior Quarterback

by WILLIAM HEUMAN

WILLIAM MORROW & COMPANY
NEW YORK, 1952

J

c. 5

MJ

To Headmaster Frank E. Gabelein, A.M., Litt.D.,
and the faculty of Stony Brook School, Stony Brook,
Long Island—the "Westwood" of this book.

CHAPTER 1

When Alan MacGregor saw the group of boys out in front of Fenwick Hall beckoning for him to come over, he had a feeling that he was walking into something from which he would be much wiser to walk away. There were three boys in the group, including his roommate, little Bertie Richards. They were all eighth-form boys, thirteen and fourteen years old, although Bertie could easily have passed for eleven or twelve.

Bertie was grinning and there was a peculiar expression in his eyes. "We were just talking about the tower, Alan," he said.

"The tower?" Alan repeated vaguely. He looked at the other two boys, whom he knew by sight but not by name; they were in his American History class. One of them was redheaded and had a very freckled face; the other, short and stout, wore a red sweater. They were studying him coolly and calculatingly.

1

Bertie Richards nodded toward Fenwick Hall and the grove of tall oak trees beyond it. "Water tower," he said.

Alan stared at him and then at the tower, a tall steel structure rising over a hundred and twenty-five feet into the air, the huge ball tank well up above the top of the tallest oak. It was painted gray and set in among the trees behind Fenwick Hall. Alan had taken no particular notice of it since arriving at Westwood Academy, although he remembered noticing, on the slip which had been given to him after registering, that the water tower and the little grove of oaks behind the Hall had been marked out of bounds.

"I don't understand," Alan muttered. "What about the tower, Bertie?"

The redheaded boy with the freckled face said coldly, "He won't do it, Bertie."

"Wait a minute." Bertie scowled. "I didn't even ask him, yet."

In the week and a half Alan had roomed with him, he had noticed that Bertie had a boundless supply of energy stored up in that small frame. He was always restless, wanting to go somewhere, to do something. Even during the study-hour period, between seven and eight in the evening, he could scarcely sit still at his desk, and he moved from one book to another so fast that

2

Alan was sure he got absolutely nothing from them.

Alan tried to smile, but he was definitely uncomfortable now. He wished Bertie hadn't called him over. "Well, what about the water tower, Bertie?" he repeated lamely, and turned his head to look at it.

Bertie Richards said quickly, "Don't look at it, Alan. If any of the masters are watching us, they'll suspect something."

"He won't do it," the redheaded boy repeated, and there was a shade of contempt in his voice now.

Alan felt his face getting warm. He hated situations like this, and he never seemed able to avoid them. Other boys knew something he didn't know, or they could do something he couldn't do or wouldn't dare attempt. He had had similar experiences at Carlson Grade School before coming here to Westwood. They were always happening to him and he was always coming off second-best.

"How do you know I won't do it?" he said with some exasperation. "You haven't even told me what it is."

The boy with the red sweater explained briefly. "Bertie's climbing to the top of the water tower tonight after study hour. He wants to know if you'll make the climb with him."

Alan felt his knees getting weak. He stood there,

3

staring at the boy in the red sweater and then at Bertie Richards, who was watching his face expectantly. He turned his head a little to look at the tower, and it seemed to have grown tremendously since he had glanced at it a few seconds ago. It was way up there in the swiftly moving clouds of this gray September day. A tiny, narrow steel ladder on the outside of the structure reached up to the platform immediately below the ball of the tank. It was for the use of repair men and painters.

"Not all the way to the top," Bertie said hopefully. "Just up to the platform. They use a portable ladder to paint the ball."

Alan MacGregor looked at him, the palms of his hands suddenly sweaty, and a sick feeling in his stomach. He wanted to laugh at little Bertie for the ridiculous statement which was meant to be encouraging. It was like telling a boy who couldn't swim that he didn't have to jump into the one hundred and twenty-five foot depth, only the one hundred foot.

"It's—it's crazy," Alan spluttered. He had always been afraid of heights. He remembered, even as a little boy, going to his father's office in the city and looking out of the window from the twenty-fifth floor. He had been terrified. "It's—it's out of bounds," he said suddenly, grasping at this small straw.

4

The two boys with Bertie were looking at Alan, smiling a little, but coldly. The redhead said, "I told you, Bertie."

"He didn't say anything," Bertie said hotly. "Give him a chance, will you?" He looked at Alan, who could feel the perspiration sliding down his back now.

"Why do you want to go up there?" Alan mumbled. "What's the idea?"

Bertie shrugged. "You know," he said vaguely. "It's just one of those things. A lot of boys have done it."

"Climbed to the top?" Alan asked incredulously.

"Three boys from the seventh form did it last year," the fat boy with the red sweater stated blandly. "It's been done a hundred times, I guess, but it takes nerve."

Alan glanced at the tower again, and it seemed to have grown still another fifty or seventy-five feet since he had last looked at it. "Have you done it?" he asked the fat boy.

"I'm not built for a climb like that," the boy in the red sweater told him calmly. He was one of those boys who could make such a statement and stand behind it with no qualms and absolutely no embarrassment.

Alan MacGregor licked his lips and looked at the redhead. Even before the boy spoke, Alan knew what he was going to say.

"I went up last year," the redhead said. "Twice."

5

Alan looked from him to Bertie Richards' eager face. He wanted to run away from them and not have to commit himself. The whole thing was unfair. Bertie Richards would make that climb, and other boys, like the redhead, would do it and brag about it later. They might be a little afraid of the undertaking, but they would grit their teeth and go up.

They weren't like him, however. They didn't have his terrible fear of heights.

"Please," Bertie Richards was saying. "Let's try it, Alan."

Alan MacGregor opened his mouth. He wanted to refuse, to say that it was foolish and that he could never do it anyway. He heard himself saying, "All right. I'll go up."

The red-haired boy was staring at him incredulously.

Bertie Richards grinned and said, "I knew you would, Alan."

A bell rang and they had to go to classes. Alan walked, as if on wooden legs, into the American History class. He sat down in his seat near the window, still weak, fear already beginning to build up inside him. When he glanced out of the window and looked across a green stretch of lawn, he could see where the oak grove began, and then the gray water tank lifting up above the trees.

"I knew you'd do it," Bertie Richards whispered from the next seat.

Alan nodded. He heard the instructor talking, but the voice seemed to come from a long distance. Mr. Harding was one of the masters he liked at Westwood. He was a rather young man, tall, light-haired, an excellent teacher.

This afternoon Alan didn't hear a word he was saying. He sat in his chair, alternately looking at Mr. Harding's face and glancing out of the window at the water tank. A kind of paralysis was creeping over him. Even now, hours before he had to make the climb, he was getting physically sick.

He heard Bertie whisper, "Alan."

Then he looked quickly at Mr. Harding, standing up near the front blackboard, smiling at him. "The French and Indian War," Mr. Harding was saying. "The years it was fought, MacGregor."

"Yes, sir," Alan murmured.

A titter went through the room, but Mr. Harding continued to smile. "That was a question, MacGregor," he said.

Alan reddened. "I'm sorry, sir," he apologized. He answered the question and noticed that Mr. Harding looked at him curiously before going on with the lesson.

When the period was over and they were moving out

7

of the room to the next class, Mr. Harding motioned to Alan to wait. When Alan came over to the desk, he said, "You all right, MacGregor? You don't look well."

"I'm all right, sir," Alan said quickly. "I'm sorry I wasn't listening, sir."

Mr. Harding toyed with the pencil in his hand. "Getting along all right at Westwood, MacGregor?" he said.

"Yes, sir," Alan told him.

"Going out for football?"

"No, sir," Alan said. "Tennis."

He saw Mr. Harding lift his eyebrows a little, and he knew the reason why. It wasn't because he particularly cared for tennis that he had gone out for the tennis team; it was a requirement at Westwood that every boy should participate in some sport. Alan didn't like football at all.

"I saw your dad and your uncle play at State," Mr. Harding was saying. "They were great. Your father was All-American one year, wasn't he?"

"Yes, sir." Alan nodded. His Uncle Jim had been All-American that same year. The MacGregors of State and, before that, of Westwood Academy were immortal. Scott MacGregor's scoring records still stood at Westwood. He was the greatest halfback the school had ever seen or ever would see. Jim MacGregor had been the greatest lineman—a big, slashing fellow with no fear in him.

Mr. Harding was smiling. "I thought you'd go out for football, MacGregor, with a name like that. You're a fairly tall boy, too. You'll be filling out in a year or two. How old are you?"

"Thirteen, sir," Alan said. He didn't like football and had never played it. He wasn't particularly keen on any sports and he wished people were not always expecting him to be a great athlete like his father or his uncle. The MacGregors were a legend at Westwood. Their names were on the honor rolls in the corridor of Fenwick Hall, inscribed in bronze: *The Boy Who Did the Most for Westwood in 19—*. Scott's name was up there for one year and big Jim's for the next.

"I'm handling the junior varsity team this year," Mr. Harding went on, "and we have a pretty stiff schedule. We're always short of material. Any time you change your mind about football, come around and see me, MacGregor."

"Yes, sir." Alan nodded. "Thank you, sir."

He went out, and found Bertie Richards waiting for him anxiously. "He suspect anything?" Bertie wanted to know. "He may have seen us looking at the tower before class."

"No," Alan murmured. "It's all right."

They went on to the next class and he managed to sit through it. It seemed hours long, but he dreaded the moment when the bell would ring and it would be over. Each hour brought him closer to the moment when he would have to stand at the foot of that slim ladder reaching up into the sky.

The English class was the last class of the afternoon, and Alan headed for the gym to get into his slacks and sweat shirt. Although the tennis season didn't start till next spring, most of the boys who went out for tennis practiced on the courts all through the fall until bad weather forced them to stop.

The gym door opened as Alan drew near it, and he stepped aside to let a half-dozen members of the varsity football team trot by. They looked big and impressive in their silver-and-blue uniforms—blue jerseys, silver pants, blue-and-white-striped stockings.

George Prescott, captain of the varsity and an end, came out last. He was a tall, rangy boy, who had been voted honor man of the school the previous year. He glanced at Alan, standing at one side of the door, and nodded and smiled pleasantly as he went by. He was a nice-looking fellow, with dark, curly hair and dark eyes. When he smiled he meant it.

Just looking at him, Alan felt a little better; he wondered how it must feel to be like George Prescott and

10

never have any fears. He could imagine Prescott going up and down that water-tank ladder the way a man goes up and down the stairs in his own home.

Coming out of the gym fifteen minutes later, Alan walked down to the tennis courts. He practiced for a while with another boy, and once when he walked over to the water cooler for a drink, he watched the football squads far across the field: the varsity, all wearing the same type of uniform, smooth and efficient as they went through the maneuvers; and the junior varsity, a small squad of less than fifteen under Mr. Harding, in a varied assortment of sweat shirts, jerseys, pants, and socks.

Alan watched a football soar up into the air and then he went back to the tennis courts. He sat down on the bench for a while, and when he lifted his head he looked at the water tower at the other end of the school grounds. He wondered bitterly why he had said he would attempt the climb. Already, he could see himself far up near the top, groping for one rung at a time, his hands clammy, unable to hold on to the cold, slippery metal, and then falling—falling.

The boy he had been playing with said from the other end of the bench, "You sick, MacGregor?"

"No," Alan muttered. "I'm all right."

He went back to the gym after a while and took his

shower. Then he went up to his room in Wharton Hall and changed to another sport coat and tie. He remembered then that he was to wait on his table tonight, and the very thought of that also made him nervous.

His turn had come up the second day at Westwood, and he had nearly spilled the big silver bowl of vegetable soup as he carried it from the kitchen to his table at the other end of the dining room. He disliked table service, but it was compulsory at Westwood.

Bertie Richards came into the room as Alan was adjusting his tie. Little Bertie was going out for basketball and he had been in the gym all afternoon after classes. He came in whistling, and Alan glanced at him in the mirror.

"Hope we have spaghetti for supper," Bertie said. "I could eat a barrel of it."

Alan just looked at him. Bertie was thinking of food. The very thought of food tonight made Alan feel nauseated. He was wondering how he could get some of it down, so the master at the table wouldn't ask him questions.

Sitting on the edge of a chair, Alan said slowly, "Aren't you worried at all, Bertie?"

Bertie looked at him. "Worried?" he asked. "About what?"

12

"Never mind," Alan said wearily.

At six o'clock they went down to the dining room. There were seven boys at each table and one master. The masters were changed constantly, so that each night a different master presided at each table. Alan saw that old Mr. Caswell, the mathematics teacher, was at his table as he left for the kitchen with the other servers.

Mr. Caswell was the monitor on their floor in the dormitory, and Bertie Richards had said on the way down from their room, "We won't have any trouble slipping out of the back door right after study period. We should be back before he starts to make his check of the rooms."

"Who's going with us?" Alan had asked him.

"Ferguson and Charlie Adams," Bertie said. "They're on our floor."

Adams, Alan had learned, was the fat boy in the red sweater and Ferguson was the redhead.

Alan, standing in line with the other table servers in the kitchen, was poignantly aware of the fact that in a little over two hours he would have to start that walk out to the water tower.

He came back with his bowl of pea soup and placed it on the table in front of Mr. Caswell. The gray-

13

headed little man with the bright blue eyes filled the individual plates and handed them around to the boys at the table.

Bertie Richards sat at Alan's elbow as they ate. He ate noisily and lustily. Alan glanced at him enviously as he himself lifted one reluctant spoonful and then another to his mouth.

Mr. Caswell said in his usual brusque manner, "Aren't you hungry, MacGregor?"

"No—no, sir," Alan muttered.

"Sick?" Caswell snapped.

"No, sir," Alan told him.

"Then eat." Mr. Caswell smiled.

"Yes, sir," said Alan. He forced a few more spoonfuls down and then got up and went to the kitchen with the plates. He came back with a huge silver platter full of spaghetti, and Bertie Richards' eyes glistened.

Alan sat there, eying the platter as Mr. Caswell filled the plates and passed them around. He listened to the hum of talk in the room and the clatter of dishes and pots and pans from the kitchen. He couldn't think. He was finding it difficult even to breathe properly. It was as if the four walls were closing in around him, compressing him, and he wanted to run away but there was no door, no window.

14

He heard Bertie Richards say, "May I have some more spaghetti, sir?"

Little Mr. Caswell filled his plate again, his blue eyes twinkling. He said genially, "It looks to me as if you are building up a tremendous amount of energy, Richards. Are you, perhaps, contemplating some gigantic effort—like climbing the water tower?"

Bertie Richards had a mouthful of bread. He started to choke on it, and his face turned red. Ferguson, who sat next to him, had to pound his back.

When Bertie finally recovered, though still red in the face and gasping for breath, little Mr. Caswell said blandly, "I was not aware that I had so devastating a sense of humor. My apologies, Richards."

Little Bertie nodded, tears still in his eyes. He looked across at Alan, who was sitting very stiff and straight, staring down at his plate. They were all glad when supper was over and they could go to their rooms.

"Whew! That was close," Bertie said, when he had closed the door behind them. "I thought at first that he suspected something, Alan. We're safe, though."

Alan sat at his desk, looking down at his books. He almost had to laugh at the thought. So they were safe! And that meant that in another hour they would have to start climbing a narrow steel ladder which went one hundred feet almost straight into the air.

15

His back was turned toward Bertie Richards as he opened a history book for the hour of study which preceded the leisure period. He closed his eyes for a moment and then he opened them again. He almost wished that he were dead.

CHAPTER 2

THE DRY AUTUMN LEAVES rustled underfoot as the boys pushed through the small grove of trees surrounding the water tower. There was a wind blowing, driving the clouds before it, sweeping them across the face of the moon, making alternate periods of light and darkness.

Overhead, tree branches squeaked and groaned, and there seemed to be a kind of singing sound high up near the top of the tower. It was the wind singing through the heavy cables, Alan MacGregor knew, but his imagination made it something worse—his own screams as he fell through space after losing his grip on those cold iron rungs.

Ferguson was saying, "It's not so bad. You just start climbing and you keep going. Don't stop and don't look down."

"What'll happen," Bertie Richards asked him, "if you look down?"

17

"Just don't do it," Ferguson warned him ominously.

They were at the foot of the tower now, circling it toward the iron ladder which went up one of the four legs. It was dark again, and they stumbled through the low brush, Alan walking in a kind of daze.

It had been easy getting out of the dormitory after the study period. All doors were open then, and boys roamed freely from one room to another, chatting, relaxing a little before bedtime.

Alan had slipped down the back stairs with Bertie Richards, and they had found Ferguson, the redhead, and Charlie Adams, the fat boy, waiting for them in the shadows outside. Already, by stepping outside the dormitory, they had broken a rule and would be given a demerit if they were caught. That would mean they would have to stay in the study room on Saturday afternoon, their usual free time.

By entering the grove around the water tower they were out of bounds, which meant another demerit, possibly two or three, because they were out of bounds after eight in the evening, an almost unpardonable sin for eighth-form boys. If they were caught now, they would lose a whole Saturday or possibly two Saturdays, and the real transgression had not yet begun.

They stood at the foot of one of the stanchions, which were set in concrete. The narrow iron ladder

18

ran up the stanchion at about a ninety-degree angle. When the moon was out of sight, Alan could only see fifteen or twenty feet up the ladder. Beyond was blackness.

Ferguson, who apparently considered himself in charge of the affair, said briskly, "Who's going first?"

Alan opened his mouth to speak, but he couldn't. He stood there, rooted to the ground, the palms of his hands sweating, no strength in his body. He heard Bertie Richards say, in a not too steady voice, "It was my idea. I'll start up. Alan can come behind me."

"That all right, MacGregor?" Ferguson asked.

Alan heard himself say in a low, husky voice, "All right."

"Here," Ferguson said to him. He was holding out his hand. "Chalk. You're supposed to write your name on the side of the tank when you reach the platform."

Alan took the small piece of white chalk from Ferguson's hand and dropped it into his pocket.

"Be windy up there," Ferguson was saying carelessly. "Hang on after you get halfway up."

"We will." Bertie Richards laughed nervously. He stepped up on the concrete base and reached for the first rung of the ladder.

"And don't look down," Ferguson warned again.

19

Bertie Richards started up, not too fast but very steadily. Alan watched him, petrified, until he was out of sight, and then he heard Ferguson say, "All right, MacGregor."

Charlie Adams, the fat boy, stood by, munching peanuts, cracking the shells. Alan could hear his teeth working on the nuts. Adams said thoughtfully, "Pretty high."

"You going?" Ferguson said to Alan.

Alan walked forward woodenly. He stepped up on the concrete base and then reached for the rung. It felt cold, hard, and very smooth.

"Best way," Ferguson told him, "is not to look down, and keep going. Don't stop until you're on the platform."

Gripping the rung with both hands, Alan MacGregor wondered how he had gotten here. He wondered why it was that things had to work out like this. The foot of this slim ladder was the last place he wanted to be, now or any time. The fear of it froze his muscles, but there was another fear which for the moment overshadowed the first. If he backed down now, he would be the laughing stock of the school.

He had to go up now, if going up killed him. Reaching for the next rung, he started up. He went up with about the same speed as Bertie Richards, who was far

20

above him now, out of sight, making no sound as he continued toward the platform.

Doggedly, Alan closed his mind to all thought. He was a machine, operating smoothly, one hand reaching up and then the other; one foot groping upward for the rungs beneath him, and then the other. It was not hard if you kept going and didn't think about it.

The wind wasn't too bad down below the treetops, and it performed one comforting service. Coming straight at him, it made his eyes water, blurring his vision. He was climbing blindly up into space like a man climbing out of a dark well.

He had no idea how high he had gone until the wind started to tug at him with more persistence, and the horrible thought came to him that he was already way up near the tops of the tall oaks in the grove. The wind was singing through the cables, and the branches were creaking, but they were *below* him now!

He stopped climbing, his body tense against the iron rungs, holding on tightly. He closed his eyes and when he opened them again, his vision was cleared. The wind brushed away some fragmentary clouds, and the moon slid out into a stretch of clear sky.

He could see. He saw first of all the other three uprights supporting the huge ball of the tank above. When he tilted his head slightly and looked up to see

21

how close he was to the platform, he was appalled to find that he was more than halfway to the top.

The ladder above him was empty, which meant that Bertie Richards had reached the platform and was waiting for him. He had to go on again almost as far as he had come.

It was then that panic hit him. He choked down the wild impulse to scream. Those smooth iron rungs became like glass, and he felt that he could not hold on to them. Already, he could feel himself falling headlong through space.

Putting his face against the rung, he closed his eyes again, and then the strength left his body. He wanted to start down, to give it up, but his arms and legs were paralyzed.

He heard Bertie Richards' voice, coming from a long way off. "Alan—Alan. What's the matter?"

The wind started to blow harder, tugging at his body, trying to tear him from the ladder. A low, startled cry broke from his lips, and he put one arm between two rungs, gripping a lower rung with the right hand. He wedged his slender frame against the rungs and kept his eyes closed.

From above, Bertie Richards, knowing something had gone wrong, was pleading. "Alan—you have to come up!"

22

At the base of the ladder, Ferguson called, "You all right, MacGregor?"

He couldn't speak to either one of them. Fear was a cold snake wrapped around his heart.

"Alan—Alan!" Bertie Richards pleaded.

"Hey—MacGregor!" Ferguson called, alarm coming into his voice too.

"You can't stay there," Bertie insisted. "You hear me, Alan?"

Alan opened his eyes and looked up. The clouds had swept across the face of the moon again, and he could see nothing. There was only the dim, vast outline of the tank ball. The ladder ten feet above him was lost. Bertie Richards and the platform were lost, and he was suspended in space.

It was like a horrible nightmare when you woke up screaming, perspiring, trying to get away from something, or you were perched on a high ledge and you felt yourself beginning to fall. This was real, though, and no matter how hard Alan MacGregor tried to imagine it was a dream, he knew that it was real.

He felt as if he were destined to stay up here the rest of his life, and there was nothing anyone could do about it. Bertie Richards couldn't help him from above, and Ferguson couldn't help him from below. He knew that he couldn't help himself.

23

Bertie Richards was calling from the platform, but his words were being swept away by the wind now. Alan clung to the ladder, his eyes closed. He didn't know how long he stayed there. It seemed like hours. He lost all track of time, and then he heard a quiet, confident voice a few feet below him.

"All right, MacGregor. Nothing to worry about."

He felt someone touching his ankle and then coming up on the outside of him, cradling his body so that he could not fall backward. He opened his eyes then and turned his head to look. The voice sounded strangely familiar. It wasn't someone he knew well, but he had heard the voice on the campus and in the corridors.

"Just relax, MacGregor. We're going down slowly. There's nothing to be afraid of."

He mumbled, "All right."

"I'll stay on the outside of you and one rung below," the voice went on calmly. "You can't fall."

He felt a little confidence come back to him. He didn't say anything, but he relaxed that vise-like grip on the rungs and reached down experimentally for the rung below.

Two strong arms supported him on either side, the hands holding to the sides of the ladder, sliding down as he descended rung by rung. They went slowly, because it was an awkward business, and all the while the voice

24

behind him kept saying, "There's nothing to worry about. We'll be down in a minute."

Then quite suddenly he felt his foot leave the rung and touch the concrete base. His rescuer held his arm as he stepped off the base to the ground, and he stood there, still shaking, unable to speak.

When he turned around he looked into the face of George Prescott, the varsity football captain. Prescott said to Ferguson, who was standing a few feet away, "Who's up there?"

"Bertie Richards, sir," Ferguson told him.

Prescott looked at Alan. "You all right now, MacGregor?" he asked.

"Yes, sir," Alan mumbled.

He heard little Bertie coming down the ladder, and then Bertie's perplexed voice. "What happened, Alan?"

Alan had no words to answer him, and Prescott knew it. The football captain said quietly, "If you boys don't want to lose several Saturdays, you'd better get back to your rooms as quickly as you can. You've got about five minutes before lights out."

He put a hand on Alan's shoulder and gave it a little squeeze. "You'll be all right in a few minutes, MacGregor. That's a pretty stiff climb."

"Yes, sir," Alan muttered, "and—and thanks for coming up for me."

25

"Forget it," Prescott said. "I just happened to be passing by and I heard these fellows calling to you."

He left them, and Alan watched him for a moment walking through the grove, heading toward the older boys' dormitory.

Ferguson said, "We'd better get back. You get your name on the tank, Richards?"

"I wrote it on," Bertie said proudly.

None of them spoke to Alan as they walked through the trees and out on the campus. Alan noticed that Bertie glanced at him every once in a while. Bertie didn't speak to him, though, until they had slipped up the back stairs, parted with Ferguson and the fat boy, and were back in their room with the door closed. Then Bertie said with anxiety in his voice, "You all right, Alan?"

"I'm all right." Alan nodded. He sat down on the edge of his bed, his face still pale, and started to take off his shoes. His hands were trembling.

"It wasn't so bad," Bertie was saying, "once you got up there. It made you feel pretty good."

Alan didn't say anything. Only now the full meaning of what he had done was beginning to creep over him. Ferguson and Charlie Adams were undoubtedly telling their roommates about it now. By morning, the whole school would know about it. Alan MacGregor, an eighth-form boy, had frozen up on the water-tower ladder. He had had to be practically carried down by George Prescott. He had been afraid.

"Maybe," Bertie said consolingly, "you can try it some other time, Alan."

They would be looking at him in the classrooms, on the campus, in the dining room. They would be looking at him all the time, whispering slyly about him. When friends or relatives came to the school, they would point him out—the boy who had climbed halfway up the water tower and then could neither get up nor down.

"Wasn't so bad," Bertie kept on saying in that maddening voice. "If you didn't stop, and kept on going—"

"Shut up," Alan shouted. "Do you hear me? Shut up—shut up—shut up!"

Bertie Richards looked bewildered. "What?" he asked blankly.

"Shut up," Alan MacGregor screamed. Then he put his face down into the pillow and cried.

CHAPTER 3

At BREAKFAST the next morning Mr.
Harding was at their table, and Alan sat at Mr. Harding's right, glad, at least, that he didn't have to serve at
this meal.

The other boys were looking at him. He kept his
eyes fastened upon a spot at the center of the table. He
didn't look around, but he knew they were looking at
him. They were talking, too. He could hear them
whispering. The story was going from one table to the
next.

"You're not eating, MacGregor," Mr. Harding said.
"Feel all right?"

"Yes, sir," Alan said. He ate his cereal, but it was
tasteless. He scarcely knew that he was eating, and it
was then that the idea came to him, and for the rest of
the meal it absorbed all his attention. He didn't care
any more that they were looking at him and talking
about him and laughing at him. He didn't care, because

28

it wasn't going to be for long. This was Saturday, and by noon he would be free. No one would be able to check up on him till suppertime, and by then he might be a hundred miles away.

Bertie Richards, who was sitting next to him at the table, said cautiously, "You feel all right now, Alan?"

"I'm all right," Alan nodded.

"I was worried last night," Bertie said, relieved. "I didn't want to make you mad, Alan."

"That's all right," Alan assured him. He was suddenly far above all these petty little things: the school and classes and boyhood friendships. He was a man. This afternoon he was leaving to make his own way in the world. He expected it to be hard at first. He might have to suffer and live in attics, and wear poor clothing, and live on a few pieces of bread, but in the end it would turn out all right. When he came back East, a successful executive, his father would treat him as an equal business associate.

His parents would regret, of course, that he had found it necessary to run away from school, but they would understand after a while that it had all been for the good.

He would come back for a visit to Westwood, and he would have his chauffeur drive up the long, tree-lined gravel road from the main highway, and the Westwood

29

boys would stare at him as he got out of his black touring car, the chauffeur opening the door for him.

They would watch him chat casually with Headmaster Warburton on the steps of Fenwick Hall before going inside, and possibly that evening he would give a talk to the boys of the school in the assembly hall, and Mr. Warburton would introduce him as that successful young executive from the Middlewest, who had spent an all too brief period of his boyhood at Westwood Academy.

Mr. Harding was saying to him, "The junior team is playing this afternoon after the varsity game, Mac-Gregor. I wish you'd stay around and watch them."

"Yes, sir," Alan murmured, and he wanted to laugh, because it was so ridiculous. He was a young executive. He had estates, a yacht, luxurious automobiles, and Mr. Harding was talking about the junior varsity team, thirteen- and fourteen-year-old boys.

They had a few classes that morning, and then after lunch most of the boys started to troop down to the football field. Visitors were arriving for the game. Walking across the campus to his dormitory, Alan saw the visiting Wharton Academy team, a laughing, boisterous group of boys clambering from their bus, going into the gymnasium to put on their uniforms.

Bertie Richards was changing into his old clothes

when Alan entered the room. "Think we'll beat Wharton, Alan?"

Alan shrugged. He changed into old clothes too, knowing that it was likely to be quite dusty and dirty inside a freight car.

"You're coming down to the game, aren't you?" Bertie asked curiously.

Again Alan shrugged mysteriously.

Little Bertie stared at him. "What's up?"

"Nothing," Alan told him. "You go on down to your little old football game."

Bertie scowled at him. "It's a good thing," he said sarcastically, "that little old George Prescott went up that ladder last night to bring you down. Guess you'd still be up there."

When Bertie left, Alan's cheeks were still red and there was an angry light in his eyes.

It was past one o'clock in the afternoon when Alan went downstairs and started across the campus. With the varsity game scheduled for one-thirty, the crowd was already down at the field and the campus quite deserted.

Alan carried only a few things wrapped in a paper bag, and he had two dollars in his pockets, most of it the money he had saved from his allowance the first week at school. It wasn't a great deal, but it would

31

have to do until he started to earn money for himself.

On his route he had to pass directly by the water tower and as he skirted the little grove of oak trees, he glanced up at the steel structure, some of the fear of the previous evening coming back to him. The tower seemed to take on human proportions. It was a great monster which had defeated him, driven him out of school.

Beyond the tower he entered the woods, taking one last look behind him to make sure no one had seen him. He had to go about a quarter of a mile through the woods before he came to the fence which marked the limits of the school property. When he stepped over the fence he was out of bounds and subject to penalty.

Another fifty yards beyond the fence, he came to the highway. The railroad track lay on the other side of the highway, and the siding at which the boxcar was stationed was a short distance back in the direction of the school.

Alan waited until the highway was clear of cars, and then he crossed rapidly, disappearing into the woods on the other side. When he reached the tracks and started back along them toward the siding, he felt his heart beginning to beat faster, and the first feeling of fear came to him. He was actually running away now. Before, he had been planning it in his mind, and that had given him pleasure. This was different.

When he saw the boxcar on the siding he became almost physically ill, and he had to fight down the impulse to turn around and retrace his steps to the campus. No one knew he was gone as yet, and they wouldn't know until suppertime when his seat at the table was empty.

He could imagine the flurry of excitement, the hum of talk around the tables. Several of the masters would leave in their cars to make a quick survey of the vicinity. The police might be notified and there would be a long-distance call to his parents. His father would come the next morning, and the search would continue, but by that time he would be hundreds of miles away.

He didn't climb into the boxcar immediately. The loading platform was deserted, but it was piled high with sacks of potatoes. This was potato country, and he had seen the trucks rolling up to the siding to unload and then, later, the locomotive backing into the siding to pick up the car. He didn't know what time the car was picked up, but he assumed it was late afternoon. There were no trucks at the platform, but he saw an old farmer shaking out potato sacks from the rear of a truck parked a short distance away.

33

Alan walked around the car cautiously. He waited until the old man had his back turned, and then he climbed up on the platform and stepped in through the open door of the boxcar.

The car was partially loaded with sacks of potatoes, and one end was strewn with empty sacks. It was quite cheerful inside, because the sun was streaming in through the open doors. The day was fairly warm for early fall, and he was glad of that because he had only worn a light sport jacket—one of his old ones.

Pushing together some of the potato sacks, he made a little burrow out of them and crawled inside, pulling the sacks over him so that he was almost completely concealed. Then he took a deep breath and relaxed. Far away he could hear the faint cheers from the football field, and he felt suddenly superior again. They were children, playing children's games, while he was going out into the world to make his fortune.

He hoped that the locomotive would come along quickly, because he was anxious to go now. He listened carefully for the sound of a distant train, but it was nearly an hour before he heard one, and he was becoming very bored just lying among the bags and waiting.

The train came roaring down, passing within a dozen yards of the siding. It made a very brief stop at the

34

Westwood station and then moved on again. Alan knew it must have been a passenger train.

He tried to relax again, and he listened to the cheers from the football field. He wondered how George Prescott was doing and if Westwood was winning. Then a truck came up and he lay very still. He heard the truck back up to the siding, and then he heard the voices of the men unloading the sacks.

A man came into the boxcar for a moment to look at the sacks already there, but he didn't stay long, and Alan lay very still under the sacks, watching him.

After a while the truck rolled away and it was quiet again. He was becoming cramped from lying in one position, and he got up cautiously to look out of the door. The siding was deserted. Even the old farmer and his truck were gone.

Alan stood just inside the door, keeping back so that no one could see him from the road, and scowled. He figured that it must be about four o'clock now and he wondered when the freight train would back up for this car. It was quite possible that the car wouldn't be picked up until after nightfall, and he didn't like the idea of sitting there all through the hours, waiting. Besides, he was getting hungry. He had eaten very little lunch, because he had been too excited then.

Once he considered the possibility of going down the

37

road to the combination lunchroom and gas station and buying a few candy bars, but he remembered that that was out of bounds, and then the queer thought came to him that he was already out of bounds and that it meant nothing to him now. It was a little difficult to get used to this fact. The rules and regulations by which the other boys lived no longer applied to him. He was free.

He didn't go down to the lunchroom, because he was afraid someone would see him and report him to the school authorities. After a while he went back to his sacks and lay down.

It was nearly dusk and there were no more cheers from the football field when he heard the freight string chugging along, heading in toward the Westwood station. You could tell a freight from a passenger string by the labored effort of the locomotive.

He sat up then, almost quivering with excitement, waiting for the string of freight cars to be broken and his own car picked up and rolled out onto the main line.

The freight string never even stopped at the Westwood station. Alan felt the vibration as it rolled by, and then everything was still again. The shadows were deepening inside the car, and he sat among the potato sacks, wondering what he should do. He was getting cold and he was hungry.

It was probably close to six o'clock. By hustling he

might be able to reach the dining room before any check was made. No one would ever know he had tried to run away. Then he remembered the sly talk and the looks, and he knew they would go on. He would still be pointed out as the boy who had got scared halfway up the water tower. He couldn't go back now.

He covered himself with the bags again in order to keep warm and tried to sleep, hoping that the freight train would pick up this car sometime during the night. He wished now that he had worn a heavier coat and a sweater, and that he had remembered to pick up a few candy bars or crackers down at the school canteen.

He wasn't sure how long he had lain under the bags before the truck rolled up. The gnawing sensation kept getting worse in his stomach, and he wondered vaguely if he would starve to death here.

Then the headlights of the truck flashed in through the open doorway, sweeping across the inside of the car. The truck swung around and backed up to the loading platform, and a man came up the steps and played a flashlight through the car. It was the old farmer. He looked at the potato sacks already in the boxcar, and then swung his flashlight toward the other end of the car, where Alan was hiding.

Alan saw the light filtering through the empty sacks around him, and then the light became stronger, and he

39

heard the man walking down toward him. He lay very still, not sure the man had seen him until he felt the sacks being pulled off him. The full glare of the flashlight struck his face then, and he blinked and sat up.

"Hey!" the farmer said in surprise. Then he smiled at Alan. "You a Westwood boy?"

Alan was shivering from the cold now and his voice was unsteady. He said evasively, "I—I have friends at Westwood."

"What are you doing here?" the old man asked him mildly.

"I'm traveling," Alan said, with what little defiance remained in him.

The farmer rubbed his jaw. "Well, you've got a long wait. This car isn't going out till Monday noon."

Alan sat back against the wall of the car. He wanted to cry now and he had to fight back the tears.

"You say you're not a Westwood boy," the old man remarked. He had swung the light off Alan's face now and was shining it on the floor of the car.

Alan didn't say anything.

Suddenly the farmer snapped his fingers. "I'm leaving now. You'd better come along. It'll be cold in here tonight."

"All right," Alan said. He had no mind of his own now. He got up dumbly, followed the farmer out of

40

the boxcar, and took his place beside him in the cab of the truck.

The old man started up the truck and backed it out of the parking place beyond the loading platform and out onto the main highway. The truck rolled a hundred yards up the highway, and Alan wasn't too surprised when it turned in through the wide-open gates of Westwood Academy.

He didn't say anything as the truck moved slowly up the tree-lined driveway. He could see the lights in the various dormitories, where most of the boys were getting ready to turn in now, and he wondered vaguely how many demerits he would get. He had been out of bounds, he had missed his supper, and he had tried to run away from school.

He was too miserable to care about the demerits. Now that he was hungry and cold, running away had lost its appeal, and coming back to the school was just as bad. He was caught between two fires.

Alan looked out of the cab window, a mist of tears in his eyes, as the truck pulled up in front of Fenwick Hall. The old man got out with him and accompanied him to the door.

They had evidently seen the truck from inside the building, and the door opened. Little Mr. Caswell came out, and so did Mr. Harding. Behind them Alan saw the headmaster, Dr. Warburton, a tall, slender, gray-haired man, who had been very kind to him the day he had registered at the academy.

Mr. Caswell just looked at Alan and smiled. "Come in, MacGregor," he said. "We're glad to see you back."

Mr. Harding walked past him to say a few words to the farmer. He squeezed Alan's arm reassuringly as he went by.

After Mr. Caswell had closed the door, Dr. Warburton said calmly, "Have you had anything to eat, MacGregor?"

"No, sir," Alan said faintly.

"Take him over to the dining room, Mr. Caswell," the headmaster directed. "Make sure he gets a good warm meal." He patted Alan on the shoulder and turned away. Nothing had been said about his running away or about his having caused the school all kinds of trouble and concern.

Alan said falteringly, "I'm sorry, sir, for having made you trouble."

Dr. Warburton turned around. "We'll talk about it tomorrow, MacGregor," he said with a smile. "Get a good night's sleep."

"Yes, sir." Alan nodded. With Mr. Caswell he walked across the campus to the empty dining room.

Mr. Caswell said, as they were going up the steps, "I

42

don't suppose you've heard, MacGregor. Westwood beat Wharton this afternoon—40 to 14."

"Yes, sir." It meant nothing to Alan. They were just numbers and names. Football meant little more than that to him.

"A great game," Mr. Caswell went on enthusiastically. "Young Prescott played the finest game of football I've seen here since the days of your father and your uncle, MacGregor."

Alan glanced at the little man curiously. It was the first time he had heard that the master had known his father and uncle.

"They were fine boys," Mr. Caswell went on. "I started my first year of teaching at Westwood when they were in their prime on the gridiron."

Alan said bitterly, "I don't suppose they ever ran away, sir, did they?"

"Not to my knowledge," Mr. Caswell told him, "but I did."

Alan had been walking across the dining room with him. He stopped in his tracks now, his eyes widening.

"It is not a matter of common knowledge," Mr. Caswell went on calmly. "My first year at Westwood, I hated it. I ran away, slept in a barn about five miles from here, and came back the next morning—quite hungry."

43

"Yes, sir," Alan murmured. He felt a little better now as he sat down at one of the tables near the kitchen door.

"It is not too bad a school," Mr. Caswell told him, "when you get used to it—and you will."

He went into the kitchen and came back in ten minutes with a steaming plate of frankfurters and beans, some warm rolls, and a cup of hot tea. He didn't stay around to keep watch over Alan. Setting the platter down on the table, he said, "The dormitory door will be open, MacGregor, when you finish. I'll tell young Richards that you are coming in. He's been quite concerned."

"Thank you, sir."

Alan sat there eating after the master had gone. It felt strange to be eating all alone in this big room which was usually filled with boys. The food tasted good and it warmed his insides. When he had emptied the big plate, the cook put his head through the door and called, "Any more?"

"No, thank you," said Alan.

He got up, went outside, and crossed the campus to his dormitory. The stairway and the corridor were empty as he went in, but the lights were still on and he could hear the low hum of talk and occasional laughter

44

in some of the rooms as he went by. The lights would not be turned out for another five minutes.

Bertie Richards had been sitting on the edge of his bed, in pajamas. He jumped up when Alan came in, his thin face warm with pleasure. He said, "I sure am glad you're back, Alan."

"I'm glad to be back, I guess," Alan said. He tried not to think about tomorrow and the next day and the day after that. In a way, he really was glad to be back.

CHAPTER 4

ALAN'S FATHER came down to the academy in the morning. After chapel that Sunday morning, a boy brought Alan the message that he was wanted in Dr. Warburton's office. As he walked over to the administration building he saw his father's car parked outside. It was no surprise to him. He had expected his father to come down, because they had undoubtedly called him long-distance when it was learned that his son was missing.

When Alan entered the office, his father stood up and greeted him with a warm smile. He was a tall man and not much heavier than he had been in his football days. Like Alan, he had brown eyes and sand-colored hair, but his hair was rather thin at the part now.

"Glad to see you, Alan," he said quietly. "I had intended to come down next Saturday—until I received Dr. Warburton's call last night."

"Yes, sir," Alan murmured. He didn't quite know

what to say next, and his father didn't seem to, either.

"Sit down, Alan," said Dr. Warburton. "We called you in to discuss a few things."

Alan sat down in one of the empty chairs in front of the desk. His father took the other chair and said awkwardly, "I suppose you know why I've come, Alan."

"Yes, sir."

"Don't you like it here at Westwood?" asked Mr. MacGregor.

"That's hardly a fair question," Dr. Warburton said with a smile, "to ask in front of the headmaster. Suppose we say, Mr. MacGregor, that Alan has had some difficulties and that he decided to leave us temporarily. He's back now and we're wondering if he wants to continue at Westwood or enter another school."

Alan felt his father's worried eyes on him, and it was another embarrassing moment. Scott MacGregor wanted him to continue at Westwood because he had been a Westwood boy himself, and it had meant so much to him.

Dr. Warburton said, "We do not think it advisable, Alan, to force a boy to remain at a school where he is unhappy."

"The first year," Mr. MacGregor said gently, "is usually the worst one, Alan. After you get used to the place you learn to like it. I had a hard time for a while

47

too, but the four years I spent here were among the happiest I've ever had. If you run away now . . ." He hesitated, as if afraid that he was using the wrong expression.

Dr. Warburton finished the sentence for him, and finished it firmly. "If you run away now, Alan, you'll always run—as a boy and as a man. Sooner or later you have to face up to things."

Alan looked down at the floor, feeling even more miserable than he had felt when the farmer led him out of the cold, dark boxcar. They were being nice to him when he had expected punishment—a whole string of demerits. They were treating him as a man, letting him make up his own mind as to his future. He said slowly, "I guess I don't really dislike it at Westwood, Father."

"Do you get along all right with your roommate?" Dr. Warburton asked him suddenly. "If rooming with another boy would help, that might be arranged."

"No, sir," Alan said hastily. "I get along fine with him."

His father said happily, "You want to give it another try, Alan, before we think of a different school?"

"Yes," Alan murmured, and he was thinking of Dr. Warburton's words. You had to face up to things—even things like the failure to climb the water tower.

Fifteen minutes later he was walking across the campus with his father. He could see boys looking in their direction and whispering—not about him but about his father, the legendary Scott MacGregor, who had scored four touchdowns once in the big game against Highbridge Academy and had then gone on to college to become All-American.

"You're beginning to fill out now, Alan," Mr. MacGregor said. "Ever think of going out for football?"

It was the first time his father had actually suggested that he go out for football, though Alan knew, of course, that Scott MacGregor would have liked to see him play the game.

"I've gone out for tennis," Alan said. "I haven't thought much about football."

"Tennis is a good game," Mr. MacGregor said. "I've always enjoyed it." As they walked along under the trees, he went on, choosing his words carefully. "Mr. Harding tells me he's short of material for the jayvee squad. Why don't you try it for a few afternoons? Football did an awful lot for me."

"I'll think about it," Alan promised. He had watched some of the practice sessions briefly and he shuddered when he thought about them. Even watching, he had flinched away from that rough bodily contact.

His father remained for dinner and left in the afternoon. Alan said good-by to him at the car, and just

49

before Mr. MacGregor released the hand brake, he said lightly, "Don't worry about that water tower, Alan. I was afraid to climb it myself when I was an eighth-form boy. When you get older it doesn't matter."

As the car rolled away Mr. MacGregor lifted a hand, and Alan waved back. So his father had known all along about the water tower! Dr. Warburton had known too, and probably all the masters, but not one of them had mentioned it to him. That was pretty nice of them.

Alan walked back to his dormitory and met Bertie Richards on the steps.

Bertie said enthusiastically, "Your dad's a big fellow, isn't he, Alan!"

"He's pretty big," Alan admitted, feeling very proud of his father. He was grateful, too, because the coming of the great Scott MacGregor had taken the boys' attention away from him and the water tower—at least for the moment.

"How many demerits they give you?" Bertie wanted to know.

"None," Alan told him, and Bertie stared at him incredulously. "I'm going out for jayvee football," Alan went on with studied indifference. "Mr. Harding's been wanting me to come out."

"You ought to be good at it," said Bertie.

50

The next afternoon Alan MacGregor learned in thirty minutes how good he was at football. He learned also that greatness on the gridiron is not something you can inherit.

Mr. Harding said to him, "When you hit the dummy, Alan, hit it hard and keep digging. If you tackle an actual runner the way you've been doing it, he'll step all over you and get away. You leave yourself open to injury."

Alan tried it again. The tackling dummy was suspended from a bar, and Alan ran toward it, throwing himself at it awkwardly. He wore a practice uniform Mr. Harding had given him, which fitted very loosely around the shoulders. He felt awkward in the hip pads and shoulder pads, but when he had looked at himself in the mirror in the locker room he was quite impressed with his bulk.

The other fifteen boys on the junior squad had watched him attentively at first, remembering that he was Scott MacGregor's son. They lost interest when they discovered he was just another hopeless dub like themselves.

"There's a great deal to learn about the game," Mr. Harding told them, "and you'll pick it up a little at a time. Don't be discouraged."

The calisthenics at the beginning of the practice ses-

51

sion had worn Alan out before the real practice session began. He had done calisthenics before, but nothing like this and never with such an enthusiastic group. When they lay back on their shoulders and did the bicycle kick with their legs, they acted as if they were going somewhere.

Most of them had had the benefit of nearly two weeks' practice and they were in much better physical condition than Alan. Many of them had played some football elsewhere and they knew what to do with themselves, while Alan was practically lost. The ball was hard to catch, and it was hard to hold after you caught it. Kicking the ball was a joke. It kept slithering off in every direction but the one in which you wanted it to go.

Alan had had no idea what position he would try out for, but Mr. Harding sized him up during a pause in the practice session. "Let me see your hands, Alan," he said.

Alan held out his hands. They were fairly large, with long fingers and wide palms. He wondered what hands had to do with a game called football.

"Fine!" Mr. Harding nodded approvingly. "You have a good pair of hands and you have the height. You can learn to be a passer, and that's what we need."

"A passer?" Alan repeated.

"Passing," Mr. Harding told him, "is about seventy-

52

five per cent of the game today. Unless you have a good passer you'll have only a mediocre squad. We'll start to work on your passing right away."

"That means I'll be a backfield man," Alan said.

Mr. Harding nodded. "We're using the T formation, and we've worked Tommy Randolph at quarterback. I'll have him teach you how to handle yourself behind the line."

Tommy Randolph was a short, sandy-haired boy with freckles. Alan knew him from his English class. He was an aggressive little fellow who hit the tackling dummy as if it were his lifelong enemy.

There wasn't any scrimmaging on Monday afternoons, so Mr. Harding had time to take Alan aside and show him how to throw a football. He had to hold it a certain way with the fingers on the laces and the thumb cocked around the other side of the ball. When he threw he had to keep his elbow in fairly close to the body, unlike throwing a baseball when you let the arm swing loosely.

Then there was the matter of the feet, of shifting and balancing yourself as you were about to throw. Alan's head was spinning as he listened; he knew he couldn't possibly remember all that Mr. Harding was telling him.

His first throws were very bad. It was almost impossible for him to get the ball to spiral, but Mr. Harding seemed pleased. "You get a good grip on the ball," he said, "and with hands like that you'll be able to control it. You have a tremendous advantage over a boy with small or average-sized hands."

Alan kept trying, throwing the ball to boys who ran out from an imaginary line of scrimmage. It seemed almost hopeless in the beginning, but with Mr. Harding standing by, correcting him on every throw, he began to get the knack of it. The elbow was tremendously important. That elbow had to be shoving itself forward with the movement of the arm, and the ball had to remain flat in his hand, pointed forward.

Tommy Randolph, who had been doing the passing for the junior team, worked with him too, and Alan noticed almost at once that with scarcely any practice at all he could throw the ball as far and as hard as Tommy could.

After he'd gotten off a pretty good pass, Tommy said to him thoughtfully, "We'll have a good team, Alan, if you can develop into a passer. Why, even the varsity doesn't have anyone who can pass well, and Mr. Harding thinks they'd have a great team this year if they did."

Alan looked at him curiously. Tommy Randolph wasn't envious of him. He was trying to help him, so

54

that perhaps he'd be the first-string quarterback instead of Tommy himself.

Alan was becoming mildly enthusiastic about the passing when Mr. Harding called a halt. "You'll have a sore arm tomorrow," he warned, "if you do too much of it. We'll work on it again next time."

Then they had a little tackling session with live runners to work on. The backs lined up on one side and the linemen on the other. One back at a time had to run forward and try to elude a charging tackler coming out of the other line.

Alan found himself last in the line of backs and he was breathing a little faster than usual when it was nearly time for him to carry the ball out and be tackled. As yet he had had no bodily contact in this practice session, but as he watched each runner go out and be hit by a tackler, the old feeling of weakness came over him.

One of the linemen on the junior squad was Ferguson, the redhead who had climbed the water tower. Ferguson was solidly built, the type that loved physical contact and any kind of give-and-take competition. He was Number Six in the line of tacklers, which meant that when Alan's turn came to run, Ferguson would be the boy to tackle him.

Mr. Harding kept calling, "Dig—dig! Don't slow down. Drive on!"

55

The boy ahead of Alan caught the ball Mr. Harding tossed to him, and he started to run with the tackler angling out in front of him. The tackle was low and hard, and the ball carrier hit the grass with a sickening thud. He looked a little dizzy as he started to get up, but he was grinning.

"Keep it moving," Mr. Harding yelled, and he tossed the ball to Alan.

Ferguson moved away from his line, crouching slightly, arms outspread like a gorilla, head tucked in between his shoulders. He was grinning, confident, aware that Alan knew nothing about running with the ball.

Alan was like a deer running along a forest path with a cougar waiting to pounce on top of him. As he left the starting point he ran as fast as he could, pushing himself to prove that he was not afraid.

Ferguson came in at him, head lowered, cleats digging into the turf. Alan flinched away from that shiny black helmet. Instinctively, he slowed down so that the impact would be less great, and then Ferguson hit him around the knees. The ball flew out of his hands, as he was lifted right off his feet. Alan was somewhat prepared for the first impact, but he wasn't ready for the twist Ferguson gave to the tackle in order to swing him

56

backward. Alan landed on the side of his face and on his nose and let out a sharp cry of pain.

When Ferguson rolled off him, and he sat up, dazed, he felt something wet trickling down over his lips. He put his hand up to his nose quickly, and it came away red and sticky with blood. The sight of the blood terrified him.

Mr. Harding came over and said quietly, "Put your head back, Alan. The bleeding will stop right away." He put a hand on the boy's shoulder, because he could see that he was shaking. "Just a bloody nose," he added casually.

One of the boys brought over the first-aid kit, and Mr. Harding wiped the blood from Alan's nose and mouth with a piece of cotton. "Nothing to worry about, Alan," he said. "It's stopping already. Better go in and take your shower now. You've had enough for one afternoon."

"Yes, sir," Alan mumbled. He was through with this brutal game. He didn't like it; there was nothing about it that he liked. Sitting there on the grass, his head tilted back, he wondered how anyone could ever learn to like a stupid game like this. He remembered, though, that when he had been practicing the passing he had enjoyed it and felt that he was progressing very fast.

59

Evidently, however, passing was only a small part of this game.

"You'll do better tomorrow," Mr. Harding said. "I'm really glad you turned out, Alan."

"Thank you, sir." Alan didn't tell Mr. Harding it was the last time in his life he would ever appear on the football field. He got up, still holding his head back, and started toward the gymnasium. Behind him he could hear the sharp yells of the players as they continued the tackling session.

By the time he reached the locker room, his nose had started to bleed again and he had to lie down on one of the benches until it stopped. He didn't bother to take a shower, because he wanted to be out of the locker room before the other players came in. He wasn't quite fast enough, however. As he was slipping on his jacket, they trooped in, dirty, laughing, their faces flushed.

Tommy Randolph paused by Alan's locker. "I think you'll make a fine passer, Alan," he said.

Alan didn't quite know what to say; he just nodded his thanks.

Then Ferguson came over, his jersey off, but still wearing his shoulder pads. He was grinning and his face was smeared with dirt. "Your nose all right, Alan?" he asked.

60

"It's stopped bleeding," Alan said, with no particular warmth in his voice.

"Everybody gets a bloody nose." Ferguson chuckled. "Now you've had yours."

"That's right," Alan muttered. He hadn't really expected Ferguson to come up, and it surprised him.

"I played jayvee last year, too," Ferguson said. "This is your first year of football, isn't it, Alan?"

"I never played before," Alan replied.

Ferguson whistled. "You passed very well," he said. "I guess you'll be the regular passer on the jayvee team this year. We're playing Springvale on Saturday. I hope you know the plays by then."

Alan just nodded. He could imagine how it would be in a regular game with the field full of players, all driving at each other with all their force. He wasn't anxious for any of that.

When he was back in the dormitory, changing to a clean shirt and putting on a tie for supper, Bertie Richards came in. "How did you make out, Alan?" he asked eagerly.

Alan shrugged. "All right, I guess. Mr. Harding said I was doing pretty well as a passer."

"Maybe you'll play Saturday against Springvale," Bertie said, in great excitement. "Maybe you'll be as good as your father."

61

Alan frowned as he looked in the mirror. He was beginning to realize that it would be quite a problem telling people that he no longer wanted to play football.
Tommy Randolph and Ferguson already looked upon
him as one of the football crowd. Bertie was talking
about the great things he would do on the gridiron.

On the way over to the dining hall he passed by the
water tower. It was dark now and the tower was outlined against the clear night sky. It was the symbol of
his first defeat, and he wondered if things would have
been easier if he had made that climb and come down
proud of his success. One defeat seemingly followed
another. He had made a mess of trying to run away,
too, and now he had tried football and would have to
admit it was too tough for him. He began to wonder
which would be harder—to admit that or to go out
tomorrow afternoon and take another bloody nose.

Mr. Harding met him on the way to supper. "How's
the nose?" he asked.

"All right, sir."

"I was very pleased with your work," Mr. Harding
said. "I've never seen a boy improve so much in so
short a time. I mean, of course, in throwing the ball.
It was really remarkable."

"Thank you, sir."

"We'll do even better tomorrow afternoon," Mr.

62

Harding went on, "and I'll start teaching you some of the plays. We might be able to use some of that passing against the Springvale jayvee team."

"Yes, sir," Alan found himself saying. He knew now that he would have to go out again tomorrow afternoon and all the other afternoons, and he rebelled at the thought of it. He was being pushed into things against his will—like climbing the tower. He had never wanted to try that, either.

He found out that he was very hungry tonight and that everything tasted much better than it usually did. That made up for the bloody nose he had gotten that afternoon, but it wouldn't make up for the bloody noses still to come, and the bumps and bruises and teeth-jarring tackles he would have to take. The thought of these was not comforting. The future looked very bleak—nothing but a series of failures and disgraces, with no victories in sight.

CHAPTER 5

ALAN PRACTICED the rest of the week with the jayvee team, steeling himself every time he left the locker room and went out on the field. Mr. Harding worked hard with him on his passing, and he was becoming quite proud of it. He was beginning to spiral the ball nicely on almost every throw. His timing was still far from perfect, but he was able to get the ball to the runner at the right moment quite often. He learned to throw ahead of his man all the time, to try to gauge the speed at which he was moving and put the ball up high where he could catch it on the dead run.

It was a different matter when he got into his first scrimmage and had tacklers charging in on him when he was trying to get the ball away. He became panicky as he retreated with the ball in his hand, waiting for the runner to get into position; and several times he was tackled hard far behind the line of scrimmage. The first few times they knocked him down he dropped the ball, and Mr. Harding had to caution him to hold on to the ball no matter what happened. That had to be drilled into him.

Handling the ball behind the center was another problem. As the T-formation quarterback, he had to take the ball on every play and hand it off to another back coming into the line or going around the ends. He had to fake it and hide it, with enemy linemen all the while trying to tear through and knock him down. It was an ordeal to remain cool and calm, to hand the ball to an oncoming player and not drop it.

The first afternoon Alan tried it he was a nervous wreck, fumbling constantly, mixing up the plays. The whole business was tremendously complicated. There were many, many plays, and they had to be run off perfectly in order to gain ground.

Mr. Harding pointed out patiently how the linemen were trying to open holes in certain parts of the line, and how the backs had to go through those holes at exactly the right moment. If the quarterback didn't get the ball into the back's hands quickly enough and smoothly enough, the play stalled at the line of scrimmage.

"It'll come to you," Mr. Harding told him. "You're learning the game at the most difficult position, Alan, but it's the ideal one for you. You have the height and you have good hands for ball handling. It'll come."

65

Alan didn't think it ever would. He wished he were an obscure lineman, but then when he saw the pile-up after a line play he wasn't sure.

Tommy Randolph helped him a great deal, explaining some of the plays. Alan noticed that even Tommy fumbled the ball occasionally, but he noticed that Tommy never flinched away from physical contact and he was never flustered when they rushed him.

Each afternoon Mr. Harding spent fully forty minutes with Alan teaching him how to throw the ball, and it was here that he started to excel. By the end of the week he was already a better passer than Tommy Randolph, and Mr. Harding was much pleased. "We'll have you in the Springvale game for part of the time, anyway," he promised. "There's a great deal you'll have to learn this fall about quarterbacking, but by the end of the season I think you'll be able to handle yourself."

Alan didn't sleep much on Friday night. He was thinking about the game next afternoon. He had written to his father that he was trying out for the jayvee team, and Mr. MacGregor had called up long-distance to say that he would be down for the Springvale game.

The school was excited about the Springvale varsity game, because it would be the first real test for Westwood and Captain George Prescott. They had won easily the previous Saturday against weak opposition.

At breakfast Alan could scarcely eat anything. He went through his classes that morning in a daze and at twelve-thirty, after a light lunch, he reported to the locker room with the junior squad. The jayvee game was scheduled for one-fifteen, the varsity game later in the afternoon.

Alan got into his uniform with the others. On the way over to the locker room he had just a few minutes to greet his father and his Uncle Jim, who had also come down for the game.

Uncle Jim, another big, sandy-haired man, greeted him with a grin. "I understand you're a passer," he said. "That was something your father never could do. We didn't pass too much in our day. It was mostly slugging it out through the line."

In the locker room the squad had a few minutes before going out on the field, and Mr. Harding went over some of the simple plays they were to use. He read the starting line-up, with Tommy Randolph at quarterback. As they left the locker room, Mr. Harding put a hand on Alan's shoulder. "All right, Alan?"

"Yes, sir," Alan replied. He was glad he wasn't starting the game, because he was sure he would fumble the ball the first time he touched it.

The little wooden bleacher seats were nearly filled

67

when the junior teams came out on the field. Alan saw the Springvale jayvees at the other end of the field, and they looked very big and efficient. He mentioned this to Tommy Randolph as they were doing their calisthenics, loosening up for the game.

Tommy said confidently, "We'll beat them, Alan."

Scott and Jim MacGregor were standing along the side lines on the far side of the field, chatting with the varsity coach, Mr. Wagner. They waved to him, and Alan felt suddenly self-conscious in his uniform. He wanted desperately to make good this afternoon with his father and uncle watching, but he was sure that he wouldn't, that he would do something terrible.

He sat on the bench at the kickoff and watched Johnny Wilson, the halfback for Westwood, catch the ball and run it up to the thirty-yard line. Tommy Randolph called them back into the huddle, and then they moved out of it into position for the first play.

Alan felt his throat getting dry. He sat there, imagining himself in on the play to be used—and making the right decisions. Even here, sitting on the bench, his mind was muddled, his arms and legs watery. Deep down inside of him he knew he was going to drag the MacGregor name through the mud this afternoon.

The first Westwood play went into the line, with Ben Summers, the fullback, carrying. Tommy Ran-

68

dolph handed him the ball smoothly, and Ben plowed into the line for about two yards.

The Springvale line was on top of him when he went down, but Summers jumped up grinning when the referee pulled the players off him. Alan wondered how he could do it. He knew that if all those players had jumped on him he would have been finished for the afternoon.

Tommy Randolph tried Chuck Wright, the halfback, around the left end, and Chuck made no gain. Then Tommy tried to throw a pass, but it wasn't good, and they kicked on the last down.

Mr. Harding came back from the side lines and sat down next to Alan. "While you're on the bench, Alan," he said, "watch everything. Notice the way the opposing line forms, the position of their backfield men on the defense. If the defensive backs play deep, you can throw short passes over the line. If they're up close, move them back with long passes. Then you cross them up with running plays so they never know what's coming."

"Yes, sir," Alan said.

How he admired Tommy Randolph standing there coolly behind the center, calling the numbers, reaching down for the ball, and then turning calmly to fake and hand it to a runner!

Mr. Harding said, "I'll put you in for a few minutes near the end of the half, Alan, just to get used to things. You'll work the very simple Series A plays."

Alan had to concentrate to remember what the Series A plays were. For four days Mr. Harding had been drumming them into his head. They were simple hand-offs to the left halfback or to the right halfback coming into the line. All he had to do was spin around and let the ball ride into the stomach of the runner—something a child could do.

"We'll save your passing for the second half," Mr. Harding told him. "Springvale won't know you're a passer, and then if we need you, you can go in and throw a few quickly before they're ready."

It was no score, with the two jayvee teams evenly matched, in the first quarter and most of the way through the second quarter. Alan was sent in with three minutes remaining in the half.

Mr. Harding said, "All right, MacGregor. In for Randolph."

Alan ran from the bench, breathing hard, his heart pounding. Mr. Harding called to him, and he turned around. "You forgot your helmet," Mr. Harding said with a smile. "Just take it easy out there."

Alan went back for his helmet and ran out again more slowly. It was a time-out and there was no rush to get into the play. Westwood had the ball on their own twenty-nine, first and ten.

Tommy Randolph, seeing Alan running toward the group, stepped out. He smiled at Alan, as he passed him on his way to the bench, and yelled, "We'll get 'em."

Alan looked at the flushed, dirty, tense faces of the Westwood boys in the huddle. He was supposed to be their field leader, but he knew deep down in his heart that he was no more qualified to be a leader than a cavalry officer would be who couldn't ride a horse.

Ferguson said to him, "What'll it be, Alan?" The redhead's lower lip was swollen and there was dried blood on his chin. On every play he had been right in the thick of things, taking the punishment.

"We—we can try Number 2-A," Alan muttered. "That sound all right?"

"Don't ever ask anybody," Ferguson advised him. "Just give the play, MacGregor."

The whistle blew and they went into formation. Alan moved up behind the center, Bill Clancey. He slapped Clancey's back to indicate that he was ready, and then he opened his mouth to call the numbers. On the 2-A plays the ball was to be snapped on the third number. It was a straight buck, Johnny Wilson taking the hand-off, going over right guard.

Alan's throat was so dry he could scarcely get the

71

numbers out. His voice was weak and strained. He had his hands down when he called the third number and he felt Clancey drive the ball back into the palm of his right hand. He turned around automatically, conscious of the sudden surge forward of the Springvale line. He held out the ball, and Wilson, piling in, running low, snatched it out of his hand and tore into the line. He made three yards on the play.

A green-jerseyed Springvale lineman catapulted through the line, sideswiping Alan as he went by. Alan staggered but didn't go down.

The Westwood boys shouted, "Let's go! Let's go!"

They were ready for the next play, lining up in the huddle. There was no time to think, no time for Alan to get his bearings. He mumbled, "3-A." It was the same play to the other side of the line, Chuck Wright carrying over left guard.

The ball came back from center on the third number once again, and Alan turned and handed it to Wright. Chuck, a stocky, blond-haired boy with a perpetual grin, went through for three yards, and a cheer came from the side lines.

The cheer heartened Alan. He felt that he was a part of this powerful machine grinding down the field toward a touchdown. He had made no mistakes thus far. He hadn't distinguished himself, but he was part of the

72

movement, no longer on the outside looking in. It gave him a good feeling.

He called for a wide end run on the next play, the third down. Ben Summers was to do the running. The ball was to be snapped on the fourth call this time. They lined up again, with the Springvale linemen yelling encouragement to each other. Alan started to call his numbers, his voice stronger than before. He bent to receive the ball, felt it strike his hands, and then turned around.

In those first two plays Alan had not been touched. The Westwood line had held, giving him time to get the ball to the runner. This time something happened. He felt hands grabbing at his shoulders, tearing at him. Then a pair of arms went around his neck, and someone was on his back, forcing him to the ground. He had no chance to give the ball to anyone. Ben Summers was moving over toward the side lines, and Alan was supposed to take a few steps in that direction and toss the ball to him—a short lateral. But he couldn't run, and another Springvale lineman tore into him as he was going down. This second man hit him full force and he felt the ball spurt out of his limp hands.

He heard the yell of excitement as the ball bounced on the grass, and then green-jerseyed Springvale boys and blue-jerseyed Westwood boys were diving at it

73

from all directions. A Springvale boy finally fell on it, hugging it to his chest and grinning.

When the Springvale tacklers rolled off Alan, he got up slowly, knowing that he had committed an enormous blunder. Springvale had possession of the ball in Westwood territory, and they were lining up in their huddle, highly excited.

"Don't worry about it," Ben Summers said to Alan. "They hit you from behind. Anybody's liable to fumble the ball."

Alan just shook his head. He dropped back to his position on the defense and once, before the play got under way, he glanced toward the side lines where his father and uncle were watching. He wondered what they thought of him.

Springvale tried two passes and then the gun went off, ending the half with the score still nothing to nothing.

As Alan trooped off the field with the squad, heading toward the locker room, Mr. Harding fell in step with him. He said quietly, "Not too bad, was it?"

"I fumbled," Alan muttered. "I lost the ball for our side."

"Hold it tighter the next time," Mr. Harding advised. "Now you know how easy it is to drop it in a game."

"Yes, sir."

74

"And don't let them get you excited," Mr. Harding went on. "Stand up there and let them do the worrying."

Alan almost felt like laughing at that. He could imagine some of those tough Springvale players worrying about him!

His father and uncle came into the locker room between halves, and the jayvee boys looked at them almost with awe.

Jim MacGregor said, "Now you're a full-fledged player, Alan. You've been in a Westwood game."

"I didn't do much," Alan confessed, "but lose the ball for us."

Scott MacGregor said, "I've been hearing a lot about your passing, Alan. It doesn't seem possible that a boy could learn to throw a football in so short a time."

"Mr. Harding's taught me an awful lot," Alan admitted.

"Let's see you get them next half," Jim MacGregor said. "We don't want a scoreless tie this afternoon."

Sitting there in the locker room, Alan was surprised to realize that the Westwood team was not down on him because he had lost the ball in those last few minutes of the first half. They had already forgotten about it. It was one of the breaks of the game—something anyone was likely to do.

75

He felt considerably cheered. It had been pretty bad out there, but not nearly as bad as he had thought it would be. He had been knocked down fairly hard but he hadn't been hurt, and Westwood had made a few gains while he was quarterbacking.

Mr. Harding spoke to them before they went back to the field for the second half. He told them the mistakes they had made and what to expect in the second half.

Alan leaned forward, listening. It was gradually coming to him that he was not a lone boy fighting against a mob, but one of eleven, a unit combining all its strength, ingenuity, and power to overthrow another unit. He could understand now why his fumble hadn't been so enormous an error. It had been shared with ten other boys. They all felt bad about losing the ball. It was part of the general misplay.

Bill Clancey, captain and center of the jayvee team, came over to Alan just before they left the room. He said quietly, "That fumble was mostly my fault, Alan. I let that Springvale guard get past me. He's been pretty slippery all afternoon."

"That's all right," Alan answered. "I should have held the ball anyway."

They went out on the field, and in five minutes

76

Springvale scored a touchdown, giving them a 6-0 lead. They missed the extra point.

Alan sat on the bench as glum as the others when the Springvale fullback lunged over the line after making several long gains. Then he sat up and cheered as West-wood came back with a long, sustained drive down the field.

Little Tommy Randolph used Chuck Wright and Ben Summers as ball carriers, and the two backs moved the ball to the Springvale fifteen-yard line. Then Tommy faked a pass and ran to the Springvale three.

Alan shouted himself hoarse when Ben Summers plunged over on the next play to tie up the score. They were all out on the side lines, yelling, as the teams prepared for the extra-point kick. Tommy Randolph held the ball and Summers dropped back to kick, booting it squarely between the uprights. It was 7-6 for West-wood.

Alan was still yelling wildly with the other boys on the bench when Mr. Harding told him to go in to replace Tommy Randolph at quarterback. He went out on the field flushed with the excitement of those last few plays. When Westwood kicked off, he raced after the ball with the others. He had done very little tackling, except on the dummy, but he headed in toward

77

the Springvale ball carrier as fast as his legs could carry him.

The green-jerseyed Springvale players were sweeping down toward them, and he saw one chunky boy with a white helmet directly in his path. He tried to swerve around him, but the Springvale player suddenly lunged with a low block. He felt himself shooting up as his legs were swept from under him. He spun in mid-air and then landed heavily on the left shoulder and the side of his face. He lay there, stunned, feeling as if the ground were heaving up and down beneath him. He heard a whistle blowing fitfully and then, after a while, Mr. Harding's voice.

"Can you sit up, Alan?" Mr. Harding was asking him.

He managed to sit up, but his head was still spinning. They lifted him to his feet and he could hardly stand.

"Get him over to the bench," Mr. Harding ordered.

Two of the jayvee substitutes helped Alan off the field. They put a jacket and a blanket around him as he sat on the bench, his head beginning to clear. Then the game got under way again with Tommy Randolph at quarterback.

Mr. Harding sat down beside Alan. "You'll be feeling all right in a few minutes, Alan," he said, "but I don't want to put you back in this afternoon."

Alan nodded. He sat there, feeling sick and weak in

78

the stomach, and he didn't care if he ever got back into the game for the rest of his life. Football was a crazy game, and he didn't like it. He was quite sure that he was never going to play again.

CHAPTER 6

THE WESTWOOD JUNIORS managed to keep Springvale from doing any more scoring, and the jubilant players trooped into the dressing room with a 7-6 victory, just as the varsity team was coming out. Alan, completely recovered from the hard fall he had taken on the field, was the last one in.

Tommy Randolph, his face flushed and his eyes shining, pounded his back and yelled, "We beat 'em! That's two straight for the jayvees, Alan."

Alan nodded. He tried to smile, but it was an effort. The side of his face hurt and that didn't make it any easier. It was quite swollen.

"I'd like to see this team come through undefeated," Randolph exulted. "Wouldn't that be something!"

He ran off to talk to someone else, and Alan sat down in front of his locker. He was pulling off his jersey when Mr. Harding came over and asked him if he was all right. "You took a nasty fall, Alan," he said sympathetically. "Does that shoulder feel all right?"

"I'm okay, sir," Alan murmured.

"Good." Mr. Harding smiled. "You'll take a lot of bumps in this game, Alan, but you'll find that after a while you won't mind them."

As he started to walk away, Alan called after him. "Mr. Harding."

The coach came back. "What is it, Alan?"

"I'm resigning from the team," Alan said deliberately. "I don't want to play any more, Mr. Harding."

Mr. Harding's blue eyes flickered, and that was the only emotion he showed. He looked at the floor for a moment and then he said, "I'm sorry to hear this, Alan, because I think you would have helped us tremendously before the end of the season, and you would have helped yourself even more. Why don't you think it over a few days and let me know on Monday what you decide to do?"

"All right." Alan nodded. He was looking at the floor too. He sat there on the bench after Mr. Harding left, listening to the talk and the laughter in the room, knowing that he never would be a part of it.

Once again he felt himself sailing through the air, after the Springvale boy blocked him, and landing with that sickening crash which had taken all the strength and enthusiasm and will power out of him. Football, he was sure, was just foolishness.

81

After taking his shower he went back to the field and sat with his father and uncle. The varsity game had just gotten under way, with Westwood pushing up the field.

His father put an arm across his shoulders and said lightly, "That was quite a fall you took, Alan. You'll have to watch those blockers when you go after a runner."

"Yes, sir."

His uncle said, "And don't worry about that fumble. When they hit you from behind like that, it's likely to happen."

They forgot about him during the next few moments, because a Springvale man intercepted a wobbly Westwood pass and came up the field with it.

Scott MacGregor said disgustedly, "What this team needs is a passer, Alan. I hope next year or the year after you'll be helping them out. A team can't get anywhere these days without a good passer."

Alan didn't say anything to that. He watched Westwood on the defense, particularly George Prescott at the end position. The black-haired varsity captain was all over the field, charging in to break up Springvale plays, rushing the passer, and then storming in to block the punt when they tried to kick.

"That boy," Jim MacGregor said enthusiastically, "is

the best end we've ever had. He'll be All-American when he gets to college."

Westwood scored the first touchdown, the fullback going over from the five-yard line, but it was George Prescott who set up the play with his block of the Springvale punt, his recovery, and then a long run on an end-around play.

At half time Westwood led by a 7-0 score, and it was then that Alan broke the news to his father that he was no longer with the jayvee team. He had to come out with it.

Mr. MacGregor had said to him, "Next Saturday you'll be playing against the Wycliffe jayvee. I hope you see more action, Alan."

Alan said slowly, "I don't expect to be playing next Saturday, Dad."

His father looked at him curiously, and his uncle, who had overheard the remark, looked also.

"You're not playing?" his father repeated.

"I'm resigning from the squad," Alan said stubbornly. He was tired of being pushed and goaded into doing things he didn't want to do. He wanted to be left alone.

"Oh," his father murmured. "I—I see."

Uncle Jim didn't say anything. He moved a few feet farther away, not taking any part in it. This was something Alan had not anticipated. He had expected both of them to argue with him, to plead with him to think it over. He had half expected Mr. Harding to do the same and he had been a little surprised when he had simply asked him to consider it more carefully.

"I don't like the game," Alan said bitterly. "I—I just don't like to play."

"That's all right, Alan," Mr. MacGregor said quickly. "You don't have to do anything you don't want to do."

"I've tried it out," Alan said tensely, his face crimson, "and I don't like it."

His father and his uncle knew why he was quitting. He was afraid—afraid of being hurt; afraid of bodily contact, the spills and falls of the gridiron. He had been hurt a little and he was running away. They knew that and they were trying hard to hide the shame in their own faces.

"If you like tennis better," his father said, "you'd better go back to it, Alan. There's nothing wrong with the game."

Then they dropped the subject, and Alan sat through the rest of the game in miserable silence. He watched the Springvale varsity tie up the score and then saw Westwood go ahead with another touchdown to win by a 14-7 score.

At five o'clock that afternoon he said good-by to his

father and Uncle Jim and watched them drive away. They had vaguely promised that they would be back the following Saturday for the Wycliffe game.

He imagined them on that long drive back to the city, neither of them saying very much, never touching on the subject of Alan MacGregor, who they had hoped might carry on the MacGregor tradition at Westwood.

Uncle Jim had no children, and Alan was an only child. There would be no other MacGregors at Westwood. It was a pity that George Prescott, or even Tommy Randolph or Ferguson, couldn't have been named MacGregor.

Leaving the parking lot, Alan cut across the campus toward the dormitory. It was still nearly an hour before suppertime, and he was wondering what he would do with the time when he heard a voice behind him.

"MacGregor! Oh, MacGregor!"

Turning around, he saw George Prescott, the varsity captain, coming toward him from the direction of the gymnasium.

"Yes, sir," Alan murmured.

Prescott fell in step with him, and Alan felt quite proud that the hero of this afternoon's game was walking across the campus with him.

"Been climbing the water tower lately?" Prescott asked with a smile.

"No, sir," Alan said sheepishly.

Prescott put a hand on his shoulder as they walked along and, as far as Alan could remember, this was the first time anyone had ever done this to him at Westwood. He had seen other boys walking by like this and he had envied them.

"I've been hearing a lot about you lately, Mac-Gregor," Prescott went on, "over at the jayvee field."

Alan glanced up at him in surprise. He didn't think the varsity team even knew he had gone out for football. He said slowly, "I played a terrible game this afternoon. I fumbled the ball right after I went in, and I guess I didn't play more than two minutes."

Prescott laughed. "I dropped three passes in a row my first varsity game," he said with a chuckle. "Two of them were in the end zone. I was ready to jump off the water tower when it was over."

Alan laughed too. "It's a good thing for Westwood that you didn't," he said.

Prescott didn't make any comment right away, and then after a few moments he said, "That's what I wanted to talk to you about, MacGregor—the good of Westwood."

Alan looked at him. They had stopped under the tall trees, and George Prescott leaned against a tree and put his hands in his pockets as he spoke.

"I don't understand," Alan said.

"I've spent six years at Westwood," the football captain said quietly. "I go on to State next fall. I think I've learned a few things in the years I've been here. I've learned, for instance, that there are some things more important than yourself. It might be your country or a friend or—or your school. It has to be that way, MacGregor. If it isn't, you'll have missed the finest thing there is."

"Yes, sir," Alan murmured, still not sure what Prescott was driving at.

"I was disappointed," George Prescott went on, "to hear that you're resigning from the jayvee squad."

Alan looked down at the ground and scuffed the earth with the toe of his shoe. "I—I don't care for football," he said tensely.

"I don't suppose," Prescott said smilingly, "that George Washington particularly cared for fighting when he was asked to take over as commander in chief during the American Revolution. He was very comfortable at Mount Vernon. But he didn't let his likes interfere with what he considered his duty."

"I can't see how it's my duty to play football," Alan protested. "I've never done anything for the team and I'm not much good at it."

"I disagree with you there," said Prescott. "Mr.

Harding told me about your passing. The other afternoon Mr. Wagner and I came over to watch. We were both impressed by the way you handled yourself after so short a time. Your judgment is excellent; you have a good strong arm; you have the height and the hands of a passer. All of us feel that you could be a tremendous asset to the Westwood varsity. It's not easy to find a good passer."

Alan was staring at the varsity captain. It was a revelation that he and the varsity coach had taken the time to come over and watch him and that they had been impressed.

"Mr. Wagner is counting on you for next season with the varsity," Prescott went on. "You'll need this fall to learn the game and to take off the rough edges. You have something the school needs, MacGregor. If you don't make your contribution, you'll never be happy at Westwood."

As they started to walk on again toward the dormitory, Alan's head was in a whirl. He said slowly, "I didn't think it was that important."

"It is," George Prescott told him, "and it's more important to you than it is to the school. After you leave Westwood, there'll be other football squads, but there'll only be one Alan MacGregor. You know the motto of this school, MacGregor?"

"Yes, sir," Alan said. " 'Character Before Career.' "

"Think about it," the football captain advised, "and good luck." He gave Alan a parting slap on the shoulder and left him out in front of his dormitory.

Bertie Richards came up as Alan was still standing there, lost in thought. Bertie had been at the game, and he said, "That was some fall you took, Alan. You all right?"

"I got up," Alan said slowly, "didn't I?"

Bertie looked at him. "Sure."

"And I'll keep on getting up," Alan said with a scowl. "See if I don't."

Bertie stared at him, mystified. "Why not?" he asked. "Everybody gets up."

"No, everybody doesn't," Alan said. Then he noticed the puzzled expression on Bertie's face and smiled. "Let's eat," he proposed. "It's nearly time."

"You sure you feel all right, Alan?" Bertie asked.

"I'm all right," Alan assured him.

Before supper he had the opportunity to say a few words to Mr. Harding, the jayvee coach. He said that he would be out for practice Monday afternoon.

CHAPTER 7

THE WESTWOOD JUNIOR squad had a short four-game schedule and, having won two of the four, they were anxious to go through the schedule undefeated. The Wycliffe game the following Saturday was supposed to be tough, but the final game of the season against the traditional rival, Highbridge Academy, would be the real test.

The varsity squad was already pointing for Highbridge, working out new plays to be used in that particular game. Coach Harding, with a less seasoned team under his command, couldn't afford to overlook Wycliffe. Each afternoon he drilled the squad on the fundamentals: tackling, blocking, running off the simple plays so that they would go smoothly.

Each afternoon Alan MacGregor left the practice field tired and bruised, but he was learning. He had to steel himself to dive at the legs of a running player, but he did it—no matter how awkwardly. On the offense he learned how to handle himself at the quarterback position. Mr. Harding taught him how to fake with the ball and slip it to another runner; how to fake and fade away and then get his pass off. It was in the passing phase of the game that he improved the most. Each afternoon he remained till nearly dusk, even after the squad had been dismissed, throwing the ball to several of the jayvee players who stayed behind.

On Friday, a light practice session before the Wycliffe game, Mr. Wagner, the varsity coach, and George Prescott came over to the jayvee field, and Mr. Harding had Alan throw for about fifteen minutes. The three men watched him silently for a while and then went into a serious consultation.

Tommy Randolph said to Alan softly, "I'll bet they're talking about you for the varsity next year, Alan. Mr. Wagner's been praying for a passer from the jayvee team."

Alan laughed. "I couldn't possibly play with the varsity for about two years at least," he said, "and even then I'd be a third-string substitute."

Randolph shook his head. "The MacGregors are supposed to be natural football players," he said. "It'll be sooner than that. From what I can see, you throw a better pass now than the regular varsity passer."

Mr. Wagner and George Prescott went back to the

varsity field, and Mr. Harding went on with his own practice session. Alan continued to throw the ball down the field to his receivers. He was getting distance to his throws now and spiraling them beautifully.

When the session was over, Mr. Harding called him aside and said quietly, "I expect to use you almost as much as Tommy Randolph against Wycliffe. If you hold up, you'll probably start against Highbridge as the regular quarterback."

Alan stared at him incredulously. Mr. Harding smiled and went on. "There may even be bigger things for you in the near future, Alan, but I am not the one to decide that. Good luck tomorrow."

"Thank you, sir." Alan hoped desperately that he wouldn't do anything to discredit himself. It had always been that way in the past. Something had always seemed to go against him, turning what should have been success into dismal failure.

Next morning this feeling became a conviction. Alan was positive that he would do something wrong or fail somewhere in the Wycliffe game—and the jayvee team was depending upon him and his passes to help bring them victory.

Earlier in the week he had written to his father that he had decided to remain with the squad, and both of the elder MacGregors arrived about noon. Alan noticed

92

that neither of them mentioned his change of mind regarding football, knowing that it might embarrass him.

The jayvee squad went into the gymnasium to change into their uniforms and when they trotted down to the field, Alan saw that Mr. Wagner, the varsity coach, was with Mr. Harding.

Tommy Randolph was to start the game at quarterback, but Alan was given the impression that when they were within striking distance of the Wycliffe goal line and passes were in order, he would be going in to throw.

He sat on the bench at the kickoff, watching Westwood take the ball and drive up the field. The Wycliffe team were big and fast for jayvees, and Alan had visions of Westwood's undefeated season going down the drain.

Mr. Wagner sat down next to him on the bench and began to talk to him for the first time. He was a chemistry teacher, and Alan wouldn't be taking chemistry for another year. He said, "Keep watching that defense setup, MacGregor. It's tremendously important when you're calling plays. Wycliffe is using a 6-2-2-1, and with a setup like that you might be able to make some ground straight through the middle."

"Yes, sir." Alan nodded.

"A 5-3-2-1 defense," Mr. Wagner went on, "is stronger through the middle, because they've got the secondaries crowding up closer backing the line. You

93

might try the ends or deep passes against a defense like that."

Alan nodded again, wondering why Mr. Wagner was taking the time to talk to him now, when he wouldn't be playing varsity ball until next year or the year after.

"How old are you?" Mr. Wagner asked suddenly.

"I'll be fourteen next week," Alan told him.

"You're tall for your age," Mr. Wagner observed. "When you fill out you'll be as big as your father."

Then he talked about football again, and Alan listened carefully. He had never dreamed that the game was so complex. Now he knew that Mr. Harding had only been giving him the bare fundamentals, because that was all he could accept in the beginning. Mr. Wagner introduced him to the deeper aspects of the game, showing him the mistakes being made by both sides, pointing out the plays Tommy Randolph called wrong.

"When you play varsity ball and collegiate ball," Mr. Wagner said, "you'll learn that you can't afford to call a wrong play, MacGregor. It might mean the game." There he sat next to Alan, a big man with gray hair and horn-rimmed spectacles, a man with a quiet but impressive way of speaking, and Alan wondered again why he was taking such pains with him.

Westwood took the ball to the Wycliffe thirty-yard line and then lost it when Chuck Wright, the halfback,

94

fumbled going through the line. Mr. Harding, who had been standing out on the side lines, had turned around to look at Alan, as if to give him the signal to go in, but when Wycliffe recovered the fumble he let Tommy Randolph remain in the game.

It was no score going into the second quarter, and then Westwood moved the ball across the fifty-yard marker on another drive. When they reached the forty, Mr. Harding turned around and pointed a finger at Alan.

Jumping to his feet, his throat dry, Alan scooped up his helmet and ran out on the field. He had instructions to pass, and pass a lot, until they put the ball over the Wycliffe goal line. It was first and ten on the forty.

In the first Westwood huddle, Bill Clancey, the captain, said, "Let's go, Alan. Throw the kind you throw in practice."

Alan nodded. His breath was coming in fits and starts and he felt weak again. He had to get over that feeling; he had to relax out here.

"What's the play?" Ben Summers, the fullback, asked.

Alan said, "12-P," and they ran up to the line of scrimmage. Alan was following Bill Clancey, standing behind him, reaching down with his hands, waiting for the ball. It was a pass play to the right end, Bud Halliday.

Alan called his numbers, his voice unsteady, not like the professional bark of Tommy Randolph. He called three numbers, and on the fourth Bill Clancey rammed the ball back at him. He remembered what he had to do on 12-P. It was a simple fake to Summers, coming down at him from the head of the T, and then the fade and the pass.

Summers whipped by, head down, making an elaborate grab at the ball and then plummeting into the line. Alan fell back with the ball in his hands. He forgot that he wasn't supposed to look at Bud Halliday right away; he was supposed to glance in another direction to throw the defense off. Little Bud, however, was in the clear, streaking out over center about ten yards past the line of scrimmage. Alan threw at him, and there was a satisfying plunk as the pigskin banged against Halliday's chest. He stumbled forward five more yards for a total gain of fifteen yards before the Wycliffe secondaries dragged him down.

From the Westwood bench and the bleacher seats came a big yell of joy. The Westwood jayvees stormed back, grinning, happy, slapping Alan's back.

"A bull's-eye!" said Bill Clancey. "Throw some, Alan."

Alan's stomach had stopped rising and falling; his hands weren't sweating so much. He was still nervous, but not nearly as much as he had been before that last play. He almost ran up to the line of scrimmage and his voice was much louder as he called the numbers for 14-P.

Again Clancey slammed the ball into his hands and he faked to Johnny Wilson, the right half. Then he faded again and, with plenty of time to throw, tossed the ball into the hands of Chuck Wright for another ten-yard gain and a first down.

Again that yell rose from the side lines, and the jay-vees came back into the huddle, whooping with joy.

Bill Clancey said, "Better mix it up a little, Alan. They'll be staying back, trying to block the passes now."

Alan called for a line play, and Ben Summers, a really fine runner, tore through right guard for six yards. They were on the Wycliffe nine-yard line, second and four, with the crowd yelling for a touchdown.

Alan watched the grim-faced Wycliffe linemen settle down at the line of scrimmage. It was a seven-man line now with the secondaries up close, not sure what Alan was going to do. They were worried about him—afraid of him because of his passes! It was the first time in his life, as far as he knew, that anyone had been afraid

97

of him. It had always been the other way around.

"Call it," Bill Clancey directed. "We're going over, Alan."

Alan called for the pass play again—12-P to Bud Halliday. They lined up. He took the ball, faked to Summers, retreated a few steps, and then raised his arm and threw the ball hard and clean to Halliday in the end zone. Bud caught it, yelling happily.

There were a few moments of wild delirium then, with everybody pounding Alan and Bud Halliday on the back. It was 6-0 for Westwood. Chuck Wright, trying to kick the extra point, missed, and it was still 6-0 when Westwood prepared to kick off to Wycliffe.

Alan was still in a daze. Trotting up the field, with the Westwood boys still slapping him on the back, he ran past the spot where his father and Uncle Jim stood. Uncle Jim clenched a triumphant fist at him, and his father grinned happily.

When Wycliffe took the ball after the kickoff, Coach Harding sent Tommy Randolph back into the game. Alan came out, knowing why Tommy was going in. He was a tough and aggressive line-backer, a very sure tackler, and they would need him on the defense.

Tommy raced past Alan on the way out grinning happily, with no envy in him, and it was a very fine thing to see. He yelped, "Great work, Alan."

Mr. Harding, who was waiting for Alan on the side lines, slapped his back and smiled as he went past on his way to the bench. The bleacher seats were filling up now, and they had all seen those accurate passes of his which had given the jayvees a score. They applauded him as he sat down, blushing.

He noticed that Mr. Wagner had left the bench but was still watching the game with George Prescott out on the side lines. Then Prescott came back to the bench and shook hands with him. "We're proud of you, Alan," he said simply, and walked away.

Alan sat there, thinking that only a week ago he had decided to quit football altogether. He had hated the game. He wondered how he could have been so foolish.

At half time it was still 6-0 for Westwood, and the crowd gave them a big hand as they left the field. They crowded into the locker room, happy and laughing, still excited over that quick touchdown.

Tommy Randolph walked with Alan. "I knew you could do it, Alan," he kept saying.

Alan hadn't been so sure himself, but he only nodded and grinned, a kind of happiness running through him that he had never known before. He was standing in front of his locker, wiping his face with a towel when Coach Harding stepped up to him.

"We're all very pleased with the score, Alan," he said

99

quietly, "but when I put you back in again the next half it'll be a lot tougher. They didn't know you before. Now they know you're a pretty dangerous passer and they'll have orders to rush you. The team is giving you excellent protection thus far, but it'll be harder for them with every Wycliffe lineman trying to get in at you. I'd suggest that you fade back a little farther before passing. It might give you that extra fraction of a second you'll need."

"Yes, sir," Alan agreed, but he wasn't very much worried. He had thrown three passes in the first half and every one of them had connected. He would throw a lot more in the second half and he wasn't particularly worried about the Wycliffe line. They hadn't bothered him at all.

When the team came out of the locker room fifteen minutes later, Scott MacGregor was waiting outside the gym. He walked down to the field with Alan, his hand on Alan's shoulder, chatting with him about the game. It was the most intimate moment Alan had ever had with his father.

"You'll have to watch that Wycliffe left end," said Mr. MacGregor. "He charges in very fast. Twice, when you were throwing, he almost got around the defense man."

"I'll watch him," Alan said casually.

100

He was on the bench when the second half started, but he knew he wouldn't be there long. When Westwood got possession of the ball, Mr. Harding sent him in for Randolph. The crowd gave him a cheer as he trotted out on the field, and the Wycliffe players stared at him.

In the huddle Alan said with assurance, "We'll pass. 9-P."

"Let's run over them again," Bill Clancey said with a grin. "The sharpshooter is back in the game."

They lined up, and Alan called his signals in a loud, clear voice. He stood there nonchalantly and then he received the ball from Clancey and faded after the fake. He was lifting his arm, looking for little Bud Halliday, when the Wycliffe left end hit him from the side. He had a fleeting glimpse of that red jersey swooping at him, and then he went down hard. He held on to the ball, but his whole frame was shaken. Something else was shaken too—his confidence in himself. He was not invincible on the gridiron.

The Wycliffe linemen were chanting, "Get that passer! Get that passer!"

It didn't help matters. The Westwood team had lost five yards on the play, but they were still confident as they came into the huddle. Chuck Wright said disgustedly, "That end got around me, Alan. It was my fault."

101

Alan didn't say anything. He called for a line play, and Johnny Wilson went through for two yards.

In the next huddle Bill Clancey said, "We'd better pass again, Alan. We'll have to kick on the next down."

Alan called the 12-P play, the first one which had worked for him. The Wycliffe line knew it was going to be a pass. They dug in at the line of scrimmage, ready to tear past the blockers and flatten Alan Mac-Gregor.

The old nervousness started to come back. Already, he could see them charging in at him, hands reaching, eyes wild, faces tense. In the first half he had been a man up on a high pedestal and they couldn't reach him. He had had plenty of time to get his passes off. It was going to be different now.

The old doubts came back, and the old feeling of inferiority. He didn't belong here; he wasn't good enough, strong enough, efficient enough.

He called the numbers, and the ball came back, and he faded. They were coming at him. Three red jerseys swarmed past his blockers. They drove him back and he retreated. He tried to find Bud Halliday, but he couldn't see clearly. There was only a jumble in front of him.

He put out a hand to ward off the first Wycliffe

102

tackler, but the red jersey came in under his arm, hitting him around the middle. As he fell backward, clutching the ball to his chest, the other two red jerseys collided with him. He was banged down violently, his face scraping on a bare spot of ground. When he got up this time he was really shaken, and the Wycliffe team were yelling excitedly. Westwood had lost another eight yards on the play.

In the huddle Bill Clancey said anxiously, "We'd better try a run, Alan."

Alan scarcely knew what play he was calling. When he received the ball from center he spun around, and Chuck Wright took it from his hand. Chuck sliced through a hole at tackle, dashed out into the clear, and raced twenty-eight yards down the left side line for a first down.

The Westwood rooters went wild again, and a jubilant team came into the huddle.

"Pass," Clancey yelped. "Now we'll pass them dizzy, Alan."

Alan nodded. He didn't share the sudden confidence of his teammates. He called for the pass play, a pass out into the flat to Johnny Wilson, and then he stepped back as the Westwood line raced up. He followed Bill Clancey, standing behind the center, and heard the Wy-

103

cliffe line-backers yelling at the linemen in front of them. "Get that passer! Get that passer!"

He looked down at Bill Clancey's back as he started to call his numbers, because he didn't want to look at those red-jerseyed boys on the other side of the scrimmage line. They were still yelling, drowning out his own voice, and then the ball came back at him.

He swung around, faking to Summers, and retreated. He knew they were coming at him, and he knew there was nothing he could do to stop them. They were going to knock him down again. When he turned to look he saw blue jerseys in front of him—Chuck Wright and Johnny Wilson, and the right guard, Sam O'Neill, who had dropped back to give him protection, but the red jerseys were slicing through, leaping, jumping, using their hands frantically, tearing the blue-jerseyed men aside, coming at him.

He couldn't find Halliday and he kept retreating, his mouth open, fear in his eyes. Two red-jerseyed Wycliffe men were free of the blockers and bearing down on him. He shifted over toward the left and now he stopped looking for Halliday. He was conscious of another red jersey coming toward him from his right side —that slashing left end his father had warned him about. He didn't know which way to go and he kept falling back—ten, twelve, fifteen yards, gripped by terror. He was halfway up the water tower again, frozen, unable to control his body, his mind filled only with one thought.

He had the ball in his hand, and these boys in red were going to manhandle him because he had possession of the ball. It was the ball that was causing all the trouble, and he had to get rid of it before they crashed into him. If he got rid of it they wouldn't hurt him. They were on top of him, reaching for him, their faces distorted with the effort, their lips tight. He had to get rid of the ball. He threw it then, not to Bud Halliday, not to anyone. He just threw it wildly, blindly, not caring where, and then he went down on his back with three Wycliffe men clawing at him, rolling him on the ground.

As he lay on his back he heard the quick roar from the side lines. A red-jerseyed figure slid by, the pigskin tight under his arm, racing for the goal line. Alan's wild pass had been easily intercepted by a Wycliffe man, who was running for a touchdown.

One of the Wycliffe boys getting up from him said with a grin, "Now you're playing on our side, Mac-Gregor."

The Wycliffe player ran over the goal line with the intercepted pass, and the score was tied at 6 all. The stunned Westwood team lined up for the extra-point kick which might mean the difference between victory and defeat.

Ben Summers came over to Alan and said bitterly, "That Wycliffe guard got past me, Alan. I don't know how he did it, but he got past me. It wasn't your fault."

Summers hadn't seen what had happened. He had been too busy trying to block out players. The onlookers had seen it from the side lines, though, and had judged him accordingly. Alan knew that. He had been judged and found wanting.

It was very silent on the Westwood side of the field. Tommy Randolph ran out from the bench, and Alan trotted in, his head down. As he sat down he heard the quick, triumphant yells from the group of Wycliffe rooters who had come down for the game. Wycliffe had kicked the extra point, giving them a 7-6 lead.

Alan MacGregor sat on the bench, hating himself, hating everything, wishing he were a thousand miles away. He had done exactly the thing he had been afraid he would do all along. After doing a fine job and riding the clouds for a few brief minutes, he had been horribly and disastrously rolled in the dust.

Mr. Harding came over, patted him on the back, and said, "Don't worry about it, Alan. Those things happen."

106

Alan looked up at him, his face haggard. "I'm sorry, sir," he mumbled.

"You proved you could pass," Mr. Harding told him consolingly, "probably as well as any boy in this school, or better."

Alan didn't say anything to that. He sat there, staring across the field after Mr. Harding had left him. He didn't see anything. There was a blur of figures in red and blue jerseys passing in front of him. He could hear the whistle blow every once in a while, and there were sudden bursts of cheering, but he wasn't part of it. His cowardice had set him apart from the other boys.

He didn't go back into the game any more that afternoon. Tommy Randolph finished out at quarterback, striving valiantly to lead Westwood over the Wycliffe goal line. Once they reached the ten-yard marker, but Wycliffe held, and Mr. Harding looked back at Alan MacGregor, as if undecided whether he should send him in to try a pass.

What he saw in Alan's face decided him. Randolph remained in the game. They tried three line plays and lost the ball and the game with it. It was 7-6 for Wycliffe when the gun went off, and the Westwood jayvee dreams of an undefeated season went up in smoke.

A glum, disappointed Westwood squad went into the locker room. They had been so jubilant after that first

107

half, so confident of victory, and now the bubble had burst.

There was very little talk. Tommy Randolph stopped at Alan's locker. He said dully, "Just one of those things, I guess, Alan. They got through to rush you too much. A fellow needs time to pass back there."

"I lost the game," Alan said.

Tommy Randolph waved a hand in protest. "Nonsense," he started to say. "All of us—"

"I lost it," Alan said furiously. "I was afraid and I threw the ball away. I lost it. I lost it!"

Some of the other boys were looking over in their direction, because his voice was unnaturally high and shrill. Tommy sat down next to him on the bench and put an arm around Alan's quivering shoulders. "Take it easy, Alan," he said quietly. "Nobody's blaming you for the loss."

"I lost it," Alan persisted. "I tell you I was afraid. They were chasing me; they—"

"Stop it," the little quarterback snapped. "Now you listen to me, Alan MacGregor. In a football game no one man ever loses and no one man on the team ever wins. In football we all win and we all lose. That's the way it has to be. Now you remember that."

He walked away, leaving Alan crushed on the bench. Red Ferguson, the guard, walked past toward the

108

shower room, a towel around his waist. As he went by he punched Alan lightly on the upper arm. "A tough one," he said. "A very hard one to lose, Alan."

Ben Summers went by and said, "We'll murder Highbridge next Saturday. See if we don't, Alan."

Alan MacGregor sat there for a long time before going in for his shower. Tommy Randolph's words kept singing through his head. Eleven men lost a football game, and eleven men won it—eleven men, and the substitutes on the bench, and the coach, and the rooters. All of them lost the game when it was lost. You divided it up into parts, even though you knew you were personally responsible. That was the unwritten law of the game.

Sitting on the side line those remaining miserable minutes of the game, he had been positive that he would never play football again. Now he knew that he would. He had to play it now, because when you ran away once you always ran away. You ran away from everything, and you were a failure—in football, in life.

Dr. Warburton was right. You couldn't run and you couldn't hide—neither in boxcars nor inside yourself. You had to stand up and face things.

CHAPTER 8

On Monday afternoon Alan was the first jayvee player on the field for practice. He sat on the bench tightening his shoe laces when the others straggled out one by one or in groups. He had been throwing the ball around for five minutes when Coach Harding arrived.

Alan had watched him coming across the field with Mr. Wagner, and then Mr. Wagner left him and headed over toward the varsity field. Mr. Harding stood near the bench, watching the practice for a moment; then he crooked a finger at Alan, motioning for him to come over.

Alan left the group of boys with whom he had been doing calisthenics, loosening up for the session, and walked to the bench. "Yes, sir," he said.

He expected no reproof for his misplay which had lost the game on Saturday, but kindly advice as to how to handle himself the next time. Mr. Harding was like that. As yet, he had said nothing about the Wycliffe game, even though Alan knew definitely that he had particularly wanted to win it.

In a very quiet, almost unconcerned voice, Mr. Harding dropped the bomb. He said, "I'm afraid, Mac-Gregor, that we won't be able to use you in the Highbridge game next Saturday."

Alan's jaw sagged. For a moment he felt unable to speak, his mind dazed. They were dropping him from the squad without giving him the opportunity to redeem himself. He tried to tell himself that it was fair, that Mr. Harding couldn't take chances with anyone who had made an error like that.

He found his voice at last and said slowly, "I'm sorry about the Wycliffe game, sir. I wish I could have done better."

Mr. Harding was smiling at him now. "We can't use you on the jayvee squad, MacGregor," he said, "because Mr. Wagner wants you over at the varsity field. You are to report immediately."

Alan gulped. "Varsity field?" he repeated weakly.

"You are being transferred to the varsity," Mr. Harding told him. "I might say that this is not a hasty decision, MacGregor. Mr. Wagner and I have discussed it for some time. He will tell you what he has in mind." Then he slapped Alan's back. "Good luck, Mac-Gregor," he said, and walked away.

111

Still dazed, his stomach fluttering, Alan started to search around for his helmet in the pile on the ground. He was going over to the varsity, to George Prescott and the big fellows—not next year or the year after but now, this afternoon!

He found his helmet just as Tommy Randolph rushed up to him, a broad grin on his face. "You're going over to the varsity," he whooped. "Boy, that's great, Alan!"

"I—I don't understand it," Alan muttered. "Why me?"

"Don't you get it, you sap?" Randolph said with a grin. "You're a passer, and the varsity needs a passer against Highbridge on Saturday. They've been watching you all along. I'll bet you're the secret weapon they'll be using against Highbridge."

Other jayvee boys came over to slap Alan's back as he started across the grass toward the distant varsity field. Ben Summers said, "We'll be pulling for you, Alan. Make good."

His helmet dangling from his hand, Alan walked over to the varsity field, his doubts increasing with each step. It was a great honor for a jayvee boy to be transferred to the varsity in midseason and it wasn't done very often, but as he watched the big fellows going through their maneuvers he knew very definitely that he didn't belong here. He was much too light for this game and

112

he had had practically no experience. The varsity players had worked a year or two with the jayvee squad first and then several years with the varsity. They knew what they were doing and how to do it.

Mr. Wagner and Captain Prescott were waiting for him when he came over to the varsity bench. Several of the varsity players turned around to look at him curiously. The powerfully built Pug Hackett, varsity center, nodded to him and grinned. He was a freckle-faced, sandy-haired fellow with tremendous shoulders, even without the shoulder pads.

Alan said to the coach, "You wanted to see me, sir?"

"Sit down a moment," Mr. Wagner told him, nodding toward the bench. "We have a few things we want to talk over with you, MacGregor."

George Prescott held out his hand to Alan. "Congratulations, Alan," he said quietly. "Welcome to the varsity."

"Thank you, sir," Alan said, and managed to smile. He sat down on the bench, and then Mr. Wagner and Prescott sat down, one on either side of him.

Mr. Wagner smiled. "You had a pretty rough afternoon against Wycliffe," he said, "after a good first half."

"Yes, sir," Alan said quietly. "I was afraid. They rushed me all over the field."

113

"I know." Mr. Wagner nodded. "However, I thought for a boy of your small experience on the gridiron you did remarkably well."

"I lost the game with that pass I threw away," Alan said, and he felt George Prescott nudge him gently.

Mr. Wagner said pleasantly, "It's not unusual for a boy as new as you are to the game, MacGregor, to get excited. That Wycliffe line put the heat on you, and it was to be expected. You'll have better protection as a passer over here, but you'll never be entirely safe behind the line as you attempt to pass. The defense is able to use its hands and they will eventually come through at you. The secret of great passing is to forget about them entirely, even when they're three feet away from you. You have to concentrate upon the runner going out for the pass."

"Yes, sir."

"I suppose," Mr. Wagner went on, "that you were quite surprised when we asked you to come over here."

"Yes, sir." Alan smiled wanly. "I thought I was the last jayvee back you'd call."

"Ordinarily," the varsity coach went on, "we don't take boys as young as you for the varsity team. We prefer waiting until they've had a little more experience and put on more weight. In your case, however, we are making an exception. I've spoken to your father about this, and he has given us his consent to use you against Highbridge on Saturday. You'll be fourteen by then, won't you?"

"I'll be fourteen Thursday, sir," Alan told him.

"Of course," Mr. Wagner said, "you won't be taking over Ronnie Hill's quarterback position. Ronnie's handled the varsity for three years. But you will be his understudy and our secret weapon against Highbridge."

Alan blinked, remembering Tommy Randolph's words.

"Highbridge," Mr. Wagner continued, "is undefeated this season, and so are we. They are as anxious to defeat us as we are to defeat them. The teams, from their records, are quite evenly matched, which means that a break or a single play can decide the game."

Alan nodded but said nothing. He was thinking of the secret-weapon angle.

"Highbridge," Mr. Wagner said, "has undoubtedly scouted us or learned quite a bit about us through other teams. They know, for instance, that our passing attack is very weak, which means that they are at this moment practicing to stop the Westwood ground game."

"So you can see, Alan," George Prescott put in, "that if a good passer suddenly comes into the game and throws two or three quick passes with Westwood in

115

scoring position, it might mean a victory for West-wood."

"Yes, sir." Alan started to worry again. This was even worse than he had suspected. With the score possibly tied, or even with Westwood losing by a few points, they were going to put him into the game, with victory or defeat resting on his right arm. All the pressure would be on him as he faded back with the ball in his hands; and this was not an unimportant jayvee game in which victory or defeat didn't matter too much. It was the big game against Highbridge, the traditional foe, with the Westwood varsity gunning for an undefeated season.

"During this week," Mr. Wagner told him, "we intend to develop two pass plays which you will use against Highbridge if you get into the game. We will be saving those plays for the moment when they will be needed. There is, of course, the possibility that you will never get into the game, MacGregor. If Westwood moves to a quick lead and holds it, we will keep the regulars on the field to protect the lead. You can understand that."

"Yes, sir." Alan breathed a little more easily. He had been trying to move mountains when there was a good possibility the mountains wouldn't have to be moved.

"You'll be practicing these plays all week," Mr. Wag-

116

ner told him. "George, here, will be your receiver. I want you to get used to each other. You must be able to know exactly how fast George can run and how high he can jump for a pass. That only comes through practice."

Captain Prescott was standing up, smiling. He said, "I think the varsity wants to see the new passer in action, Mr. Wagner."

As they went out on the field, the varsity players looked at Alan curiously. Mr. Wagner explained carefully to them what he wanted done. He had Alan stand at one side while Ronnie Hill, the regular quarterback, went through the movements.

The secret pass play was not too involved, but it was very tricky. The quarterback was to fade with the ball after faking it to the oncoming fullback. He was to fade to his own right, with the left half swinging around behind him as if to take a lateral. The lateral was to be faked also, the left half speeding by holding out his hands for the ball, bringing the secondaries up a few steps. Alan was to straighten up suddenly and peg the ball downfield to the left end, George Prescott, who would be angling easily through the defensive secondaries.

"The pass won't be more than twenty yards," Mr. Wagner explained, "but it'll have to be thrown fast and

117

accurately over toward the side lines. We'll work exactly the same play toward the other side of the field and by that time, we hope, we'll be in the end zone."

Ronnie Hill tried it once, his pass missing Prescott, and then Coach Wagner said, "All right, MacGregor. Try it."

The varsity quarterback stepped aside, smiling encouragingly. He was a tall, dark-haired boy who would be going on to State next year with Prescott.

Alan stepped up to the center, his heart pounding. He glanced at the three backs behind him and then over at Prescott, crouching out on the wing. Prescott smiled at him and nodded.

"Signals," Alan said in a husky voice. "1—2—3—"

Pug Hackett rammed the ball back at him on the third count and he swung and faked to the fullback. He faded away then, waiting for the left half to swing behind him and come around for that fake lateral. He noticed that he had only one blocker in front of him as he moved toward the side lines with the ball in his hands. The thought of that was not encouraging.

He made his fake to the halfback and then stopped and straightened up. George Prescott, who had been loafing across the field, suddenly sprang into action. He cut for the side lines about twenty yards past the line of scrimmage, running with amazing speed.

118

Alan felt that it was almost impossible to hit a target moving at that rate. Flustered, he threw the ball hurriedly and it wobbled off his hand, not even reaching Prescott. Red-faced, Alan bit his lip.

Mr. Wagner said coolly, "Try it again. That's what we're here for."

George Prescott returned the ball and trotted back smiling, unconcerned. They ran the play through again, and this time Alan's pass was much better. Prescott caught it just as he stepped out of bounds. It would have been a twenty-two yard gain in a game.

"That's better," Mr. Wagner told him. "Now we'll try it to the other side of the field. Prescott will still be the receiver, but he'll be swinging over toward the opposite side line."

For fully thirty minutes Alan worked on the two plays, with Mr. Wagner correcting his mistakes, advising him. Alan didn't fake cleverly enough and he kept looking at George Prescott instead of concentrating on the back to whom he was to fake the lateral.

"We want this play to look exactly like a lateral," Mr. Wagner explained, "right up to the final second when you get rid of the ball. We'll have the element of surprise here, too, because Highbridge won't know that we have a pretty capable passer on the squad."

Alan reddened at the compliment. His passes had

119

been getting smoother all the time, and even the varsity team was a little surprised. He kept remembering, though, that this was not actual competition. There were no enemy linemen tearing in at him; there was no pressure here.

During the course of the afternoon he learned several of the other plays, which were quite similar to the ones the jayvee squad had been using. Then for another thirty minutes he worked with George Prescott and several of the second-string backs, running the special play over and over again. He threw passes to Prescott, connecting with more and more of them, until his arm started to hurt.

Captain Prescott said to him, "The secret of a great passing combination is practice, Alan. We've got to do it so many times that we can't miss. That's how these acrobats and trapeze men in the circus develop their skill. We won't have as much time as we need before the Highbridge game, but I think we'll do all right."

Alan left the field at dusk and found Mr. Harding waiting for him in the locker room. "How did it go, Alan?" he asked.

"I hope it'll work out all right, sir," said Alan.

"You *know* it'll work out," Mr. Harding corrected him. "Just remember that after you throw that first successful pass, Highbridge is going to be afraid of you, Alan. Understand?"

"Afraid of me," Alan muttered. He kept repeating it to himself as he took his shower and went over to his room.

Bertie Richards had already heard the news, and his eyes were popping when Alan came in. "You're playing with the varsity, Alan!" he exclaimed.

Alan smiled at him. "It's not really that," he said. "They might use me in the Highbridge game, but only as a last resort."

He called up his father before going down to supper and told him the details.

"We're pulling for you, Alan," said Mr. MacGregor. "Good luck!"

That made him feel better, a little more sure of himself. He was a MacGregor, and the MacGregors were known to be men who rose to the occasion. For the first time in his life he was really proud of the name and of his heritage. It had been a burden, with people expecting him to live up to his father and his uncle. Now he hoped fervently that when the test came, the MacGregor blood in him would prove itself.

CHAPTER 9

THE HIGHBRIDGE TEAM came out on the field thirty-three strong, a big, rangy outfit in green-and-gold uniforms: gold helmets and gold rayon pants, green jerseys, and green-and-white stockings. The gold helmets had a wide black stripe down the middle.

As Alan MacGregor watched the green-jerseyed team coming out across the field, he found himself almost praying that he wouldn't have to go into the game this afternoon. From Monday until Friday they had worked on the special plays, and Mr. Wagner had expressed his satisfaction with them. The Friday afternoon workout had been a light one, with Alan and George Prescott doing nothing but practice the pass. It had clicked about ninety per cent of the time, though of course without opposition.

Bertie Richards stood near the Westwood bench, watching as Highbridge came on the field. He whistled. "Boy, they're big, Alan!" he said.

122

Alan didn't say anything. He glanced over at his father and his uncle, who were talking with Mr. Wagner and Mr. Harding. They had just watched a fighting Westwood jayvee team come from behind to beat the Highbridge jayvees by a 21-14 score, and Mr. Harding was in good spirits.

The biggest crowd in Westwood history was on hand for the game between the two undefeated elevens. Bus load after bus load of Highbridge rooters had rolled up and then the cheering, chanting undergraduates had marched down from the parking lot, waving the green-and-gold Highbridge pennants.

Hundreds of old Westwood graduates were present, filling the wooden bleacher seats, standing behind the rope which had been stretched up and down the side lines. The officials stood in a little clump down near the goal posts, waiting for the two teams to finish warming up.

They were both veteran teams, mostly seniors who would go on to college and play football for a long time. Alan was proud of this Westwood squad. They looked fast, smooth, and efficient as they went through the warming-up exercises. Then the two squads moved up and down the field, running off plays.

During the warm-up session Alan did very little. He loosened up his arm by tossing short passes, but he was

123

under orders not to reveal to the Highbridge team that he was a passer.

"We want to spring this as a complete surprise," Mr. Wagner told him. "When Ronnie Hill comes out of the game, he'll be coming out because of a supposed injury, and you'll be going in because I have no one capable of filling Hill's shoes."

After the tossup, which Highbridge won, the substitutes retired to the bench and the two regular teams took the field, Highbridge defending the north goal and Westwood the south. Westwood prepared to kick off.

The day was warm for early November, with a bright sun and very little wind, making it ideal for kicking and passing. Alan MacGregor prayed that it would remain that way all during the game. If a stiff breeze sprang up in the late afternoon when he had to go in, and was against the passer, it would be too bad.

Mr. Harding came over and sat down next to Alan just before the kickoff. "Just relax, MacGregor," he said. "You can't do anything anyway sitting here, and we don't want you tighter than a drum if you have to go in."

"Yes, sir."

Alan glanced back and saw his father and his uncle sitting in the bleacher seats just behind him. They

smiled at him. When he turned his head, big Bill Lee, varsity fullback, was trotting forward.

Lee's right foot swung, and the pigskin lifted into the air, turning end over end, the Highbridge quarterback catching it on the ten-yard line. The green and gold came up the field beautifully, the blockers forming in front of the runner, and then those blockers started to go down as they made contact with the silver and blue of Westwood.

Pug Hackett, Westwood center, ripped in to take out two blockers, and then George Prescott went over the top of the three men to nail the runner on the Highbridge twenty-three.

Highbridge went into the huddle, came out of it briskly, and ran a beautiful spinner play over left tackle, which picked up several yards.

Mr. Harding said, "They're running out of the double-wing formation, Alan, and they're very smooth. It's going to be tight this afternoon."

Alan just nodded.

"Watch how those Highbridge linemen work to open holes," Mr. Harding told him. "This is the place to learn football, MacGregor—on the bench, watching."

Highbridge moved the ball to the fifty-yard line, making two first downs, but Westwood stiffened on the fifty, and the Highbridge kicker had to drop back to punt.

Ronnie Hill ran the kick back to the twenty-one, taking it on his own fifteen, and Westwood went on the offensive. They, too, moved smoothly, with Hill at the quarterback spot handling the team beautifully. His fakes were so artful that even Alan had difficulty following the runner at times, though he knew most of the plays they were using. In this first quarter neither quarterback was willing to take chances with trick plays or passes. They ran straight "bread-and-butter" plays, simple hand-offs with expert blocking to get the runners through.

Bill Lee and Skip Ledeaux, the right half, alternated in carrying the ball into Highbridge territory. They reached the forty-two but lost the ball when Ledeaux fumbled going through the line.

The big Highbridge crowd roared when the green and gold took possession of the ball on their own forty, but their roars turned to groans a moment later as George Prescott flashed in from the end position to nail the runner, who was trying to swing around the opposite end. Highbridge lost six yards on the play. They made five yards on the next two plays—running plays—but they had to kick on the fourth down.

Mr. Harding said to Alan, "Watch Prescott on this

play. He knows it's his last game for Westwood."

Alan kept his eyes on Prescott as the Highbridge center spun the ball back to the kicker. Prescott had to get by two blockers to reach the kicker, but he did so with his amazing speed. Alan was standing up, yelling, as Prescott went into the air, reaching with his hands. The ball bounced off his chest, tumbling back toward the Highbridge goal line. Scarcely breaking his stride after that tremendous leap, George Prescott bounded after the ball, two Highbridge men going with him. The Westwood captain reached it first, falling on the ball on the Highbridge eighteen, and the Westwood rooters went mad with joy.

Ronnie Hill never gave Highbridge time to get set. He fooled them completely with a fake buck over center, gave the ball to the speedy Ledeaux, and Ledeaux ripped over left tackle, straightened up when he came out into the open, and then flashed sixteen yards to the Highbridge two.

In two bucks big Bill Lee went over for the score. Hill kicked the extra point, and it was 7-0 for Westwood. Alan MacGregor cheered himself hoarse, along with the other substitutes on the Westwood bench. He felt a lot more relaxed now that Westwood was leading and it was less likely that he would have to go into the game.

Highbridge came back hard during the rest of the quarter and all through the second quarter, twice getting fairly deep into Westwood territory, but never quite able to score. Their left half was a good passer and several times his passes nearly got by the Westwood secondaries for long gains.

"He's a good passer, Alan," Mr. Harding said, "but I wouldn't say he was much better than you are, and he's probably been playing varsity ball for two or three years."

Alan made no comment. Ronnie Hill attempted a few passes in the late minutes of the half, but none of them connected. When the gun went off, ending the half, the score was still 7-0 for Westwood.

Alan followed the regulars into the locker room, his new uniform as clean and spotless as when he had put it on. Looking at the men who had been in the game, he was almost ashamed. They had played hard, tough football and they showed it.

Alan saw George Prescott nursing a bruised lower lip. Prescott grinned at him and said, "How's it going, Alan?"

"All right, sir," Alan told him. "It's a great game."

"We'll beat them," Prescott said calmly. "You be ready if we need you."

130

"It—it doesn't look as if you'll be needing me," Alan muttered.

George Prescott shrugged. "Football is a funny game, Alan. You can almost always expect surprises before the last gun."

Alan MacGregor hoped fervently that Westwood could maintain its seven-point margin over Highbridge. Then there would be no necessity for him to go in.

The squad went back to the field after a brief talk by Coach Wagner. The regulars were in the line-up, and Alan sat down on the bench next to Mr. Harding. Highbridge kicked off and Westwood took possession of the ball.

The third quarter of the game was like the second, with both teams battling to cross midfield and neither of them getting far beyond it. It was a battle of lines this afternoon; both forward walls were very strong, and the backs were unable to get clear.

Once the Highbridge left half got off a beautiful pass which carried to the Westwood ten-yard line, but the receiver just got the ball on his finger tips and then dropped it. The completed pass would have resulted in a score and possibly a tied game. Alan's heart was in his throat as he watched the Highbridge receiver strain to catch that long throw.

131

"I'm afraid," said Mr. Harding, "that they're going to connect with one of them before the afternoon's over. I hope not."

The quarter ended with the ball in Westwood's possession on their own twenty-five and the score still 7-0 for Westwood.

Coach Wagner sent in substitutes to give the tired regulars a well-earned rest, but Alan still sat on the bench. Once Mr. Harding advised him to get up and move around a little, so he wouldn't be stiff and cold if he did have to go in suddenly.

Alan took his advice. With his jacket on and the collar pulled up high, he trotted up and down in front of the bench for a few minutes, feeling very self-conscious. Then he sat down again.

Highbridge had taken possession of the ball, and the left half, who did the passing, had just sent another long one down the field. It was broken up by Ronnie Hill and Skip Ledeaux. The green and gold had the ball on their own thirty-five, third and nine, and it looked as if there would be another pass coming up before they had to kick. The play started that way, the left half fading with the ball and the Westwood secondaries picking up the possible receivers frantically—then things began to happen.

The Highbridge right half, who had been loafing in

the backfield, suddenly cut toward the line of scrimmage. The man with the ball tossed him a short lateral and he went through center, where a big hole had been left vacant by Pug Hackett and the guard, who had dropped back to defend against a short pass. The Highbridge runner tore through at a terrific rate of speed, slipped around Pug Hackett's lunge, and then cut down the right side line out in the open.

The entire Highbridge rooting section came to its feet with one sustained roar as the runner skimmed over one white line after another. He was past midfield, swinging in away from the side lines, getting beautiful downfield blocking from the green-and-gold men who had slipped through. George Prescott nearly caught him on the twenty, but the Westwood captain's fingers slipped off the runner's ankles and he kept going, stumbling, straightening himself, and then streaking for the far corner. He went over into the end zone with three Westwood men clinging to him. It was 7-6 for Westwood, with the extra-point kick coming up.

The Westwood rooting section was crushed. They sat in silence, listening to the delirious sounds coming from the Highbridge crowd. The Highbridge team was going mad as they pounded the back of the runner who had made the score.

Mr. Harding turned to Alan and said quietly,

133

"Watch George Prescott. He has to stop this kick."

Alan watched the great end again. Captain Prescott was already down in position out on the wing, the first man on either side to be ready. He crouched there as the two teams took their places for the kick, one Highbridge man kneeling, waiting for the spin-back. The kicker backed several feet.

Prescott didn't move a muscle. He was like a tiger in the jungle, poised for this charge. Watching him, Alan knew that he was going to do it, that nothing in this world could stop George Prescott from blocking that kick and preserving the Westwood lead.

They were all out on the side lines, watching, a hush settling over the field. George Prescott looked at the spot where the ball was to be set down. He didn't move his head to the right or left. Such was his concentration, that Alan felt he would not have seen an elephant if it had suddenly walked in front of him. He would have looked right through it at that spot on the gridiron.

Then the ball spun back, and the man who was to hold it reached up, caught it, and placed it hastily on the ground. The Highbridge right half was assigned to block out George Prescott, and as Prescott came magnificently charging in, the Highbridge man made a perfect block. But he didn't touch Prescott. Prescott was up in the air in an incredibly long flying dive, both

134

his hands reaching forward—a beautiful thing to behold. The kicker's toe connected with the ball and it rose into the air about two feet before Prescott's right hand batted it down.

Pandemonium reigned in the bleacher seats behind the Westwood bench. Alan MacGregor didn't shout. His throat was too full. He couldn't say anything. When he walked back to the bench and looked at Mr. Harding, he was positive there were tears in the coach's eyes.

"There are some things," Mr. Harding said huskily, "that a boy just has to do. George Prescott will remember that the rest of his life, MacGregor. When he has doubts, when he is uncertain of himself, he will remember that, and it will make him strong. That's what football can do for you. That's why it's a great game."

"Yes, sir." Alan felt small and humble.

Highbridge kicked off after the sensational touchdown, with nine minutes of the final quarter remaining and the score 7-6 for Westwood. Ronnie Hill had orders from the bench to play it safe now and he called only conservative plays, making sure there would be no fumbles.

Westwood had to kick on the third down after moving the ball to their own twenty-six. Big Bill Lee got off a beautiful, spiraling punt, and Highbridge had to put the ball in play from their own twenty-nine.

The seconds and the minutes were ticking away, with that one-point lead separating the two teams. The Westwood defense held like steel as the big fellows in the center of the line threw back the Highbridge charges. With six minutes and then four minutes remaining, the one point became bigger and bigger. Westwood was ready to start chanting the victory song, and then Highbridge broke loose. A long pass was completed to the Westwood thirty-yard line, and it was first and ten in scoring territory with plenty of time to score.

Again the Highbridge rooters went mad as their team lined up for this final drive at the goal. Westwood held, allowing five yards on three plays, and then Highbridge called time out.

"They're going to try a field goal," Mr. Harding said, "and the ball's right in front of the uprights. They might make it."

Alan watched the Highbridge kicker measuring off the distance during the time-out period. It was a fairly long kick for a schoolboy kicker but not impossible, and a successful kick would give Highbridge a 9-7 lead.

Alan's throat was dry again as he watched. He sat next to Mr. Harding, his shoulders hunched, his hands clasped tightly. The time-out period was over, and Highbridge lined up with one man squatting, ready to hold the ball for the field goal.

George Prescott wasn't going to be allowed to block this kick. Alan noticed that two blockers were over on Prescott's side of the field, watching him grimly. Then the ball was snapped and the kicker moved toward it. George Prescott came in with that same flying dive. He was reaching for the ball, but it cleared his hands with plenty to spare.

Alan stood up as the ball rose into the air, end over end, flying straight for the uprights. He knew it was going through—and it did. It passed between the uprights and several yards above the horizontal bar, a successful field goal. Alan sat down again, all the strength gone out of him. It didn't seem possible that this gallant Westwood team could lose after the amazing fight they had put up and the miraculous block George Prescott had made. It just couldn't be.

Mr. Harding said quietly, "Get up, MacGregor, and move about."

Alan realized then that the game was not quite over. They had a few brief minutes to turn defeat into victory. This was exactly the situation for which Coach Wagner had been preparing his jayvee passer.

Alan got up. He took off his jacket and started to

run up and down, trying not to think about the game or anything else. He just trotted back and forth in front of the bench, his mind a blank, as the two teams prepared for the kickoff.

Across the field the Highbridge rooters were still whooping deliriously. An official galloped past the Westwood bench and yelled to Coach Wagner. "Three minutes and fifteen seconds!"

That was all the time they had left in this game, with Highbridge kicking off and Westwood having to come all the way up the field and across the last white line.

At the kickoff, Alan stopped running to watch. Skip Ledeaux caught the ball on the eight and started up the field, but the green-and-gold team were down on him like a pack of terriers closing for the kill. They harried him over toward the side lines and he was knocked out of bounds on the nineteen. Highbridge had victory in their grasp, and the thought of it redoubled their strength. When they lined up for the first scrimmage, the linemen were hounds on the leash, hardly to be restrained.

Coach Wagner looked around from the side line. When he saw Alan standing and watching the play, he motioned for him to keep running. Alan watched as he warmed up.

138

Westwood came out of the huddle and trotted to the line of scrimmage, grim-faced, still unbeaten, determined to cover those eighty-one long yards to the Highbridge goal line. Ronnie Hill faked a pass and sent Bill Lee through right tackle. Big Bill picked up eight yards on the play. He was still on his feet, bucking to go on when the whistle blew. Five Highbridge men were holding him.

Then it was Skip Ledeaux, swinging around the end, running with a speed he had never before shown, a speed he did not possess; he had to dig deep down into the inner recesses of his spirit to find the energy for it. Ledeaux made eight yards on that drive, literally tearing past three Highbridge men. He went nine more yards up along the side line, but he was out of bounds and the yards didn't count.

Alan had stopped running again, because he had to watch this. He couldn't keep from watching it. Both sides were roaring now as the tension mounted every moment. But Westwood didn't have enough time. They had to make that distance quickly before the clock killed them.

Ronnie Hill had to dig down into the bag and come up with something special, and he did it. It was an old end-around, a play he hadn't called all afternoon. Westwood kept it in reserve for occasions like this. It was a fake to Bill Lee and another fake to Ledeaux; then the brilliant George Prescott doubled back from the end position and swung in behind Hill to take the short lateral.

Prescott was around the opposite end like a flash, driving up the field, out in the open, with the Westwood crowd going mad. He came up over the forty, the fifty, going into Highbridge territory, tearing past one tackler, deftly eluding another, down to the forty-five, the forty, the thirty-five; and then the whole Highbridge team seemed to envelop him. As he disappeared on the thirty-three, Coach Wagner turned around and beckoned to Alan MacGregor.

There was a Highbridge time-out. Alan went over to the side lines, his helmet in his hand. He stood in front of the coach, his breath coming in long heaves.

Mr. Wagner said quietly, "Go in for Hill, Mac-Gregor. You know what to do. Two passes will put us over."

"Yes, sir," Alan said. It was very simple. Two passes would put them over. He turned and ran out on the field.

The Westwood team were standing in a huddle, and the water boy was out there with his pail and paper cups and towels. When they saw Alan coming, Ronnie Hill stepped out of the huddle and came toward the side

140

lines, limping badly. As he passed Alan he winked and said softly, "You can do it, Alan."

The Highbridge players watched Hill going off and Alan MacGregor coming in. Alan felt them studying him as he approached the huddle of Westwood players. They could see how young he was. He was deathly pale and, despite the bulky padding, he was skinny in comparison with these young giants.

When he stepped into the Westwood huddle, George Prescott greeted him. The Westwood captain's face was pale too, and streaked with dirt, but there was a light in his dark eyes. "We're going over, MacGregor," he said. "They can't stop us now."

"Yes, sir," Alan mumbled.

"We'll try that 7-P play first," Captain Prescott went on, as calmly as if he were speaking at a practice session. "You move toward the right side line and I'll be coming over toward your side of the field. You've got it?"

"Yes, sir."

The whistle blew, and Alan walked dazedly back to where they were to huddle even though the play had been decided.

Prescott said to him, "Put your helmet on, MacGregor."

Alan still had the helmet in his hand, dangling from the chin strap. He had forgotten about it completely.

141

Now he put the helmet on and tightened the strap and said, in a voice which belonged to a complete stranger, "7-P."

Then he followed Pug Hackett to the center position and stood behind him, ready to call his numbers. He looked across the backs of the crouching Westwood linemen at the Highbridge forwards—the big fellows in green and gold, wearing the gaudy golden helmets with the wide black stripe down the middle. They had played magnificent football this afternoon. Like Westwood, they had never given up, and they weren't giving up now. They were coming across that imaginary line; they were coming after him with all the remaining power in their bodies.

Alan tried desperately to stop these thoughts. He had to concentrate on the play, on George Prescott streaking across the gridiron waiting for that accurate pass which Alan had to throw. He opened his mouth to start calling the numbers and no sounds came out. As he swallowed he saw the Highbridge men looking at him. Then he managed to call the numbers: "1—2—3—"

Pug Hackett rammed the ball back on three. Alan felt it come into his hands. He turned and made his fake to Bill Lee, driving down the center, and then he started to drift, running on unsteady legs. Sam Marvin, the left half, swung around behind him. Alan was sup-

142

posed to fake the lateral to Marvin, too, and then stop and peg down the field to Prescott. But the Highbridge team were coming in at him, swarming from all directions. Alan saw them coming, saw their faces, and forgot about Marvin—forgot about Prescott streaking across the gridiron. He just kept running toward the side lines, gripped by a wild, unreasoning terror, wanting only to get away.

A Highbridge man had gotten past Ledeaux, his only blocker. Alan could see his intense blue eyes and the bloody streak across his chin. Alan ran away from him and from the others behind him. Then they were on top of him and he could run no farther. He felt them closing in on him; he felt their hands tearing at him. He remembered only one thing as they drove him to the ground. He had to hold on to the ball. He did hold it —the one trivial victory in this dismal failure. Lying there on the ground, the ball hugged tight to his chest, he knew again the bitterness of defeat. He had failed, just as he had failed the jayvee team in the Wycliffe game. He had lost his nerve. Instead of rising to the occasion like the others, he had not even done as well as he usually did.

The jubilant Highbridge players rolled off him and he got up. The referee took the ball from his hands and placed it on the thirty-nine-yard line. He had lost six precious yards on the play. Westwood was hurrying into the huddle, because there was no time to waste. Alan went into the huddle too, shocked by the enormity of his failure.

George Prescott said evenly, "We have time for possibly two plays, no more. Try it again, Alan."

Big Bill Lee said, "You can do it, boy," and gave Alan a pat on the shoulder.

There was no censure, no bitterness because he had failed. Still undefeated, still confident, they were ready to try it again.

Alan had little time to think about it, because the seconds were ticking away. As Westwood rushed up to the line of scrimmage, he followed Pug Hackett. Before starting to call the numbers, he glanced back. Crouching, their elbows on their knees, Marvin, Lee, and Ledeaux, the three backs forming the head of the T looked at him, and he saw the sympathy in their eyes. They were trying to lend him their strength and their courage. They understood that he was young and inexperienced; they were aware of the tremendous pressure on him. The linemen knew too, and so did Coach Wagner and the Westwood rooters. They all knew and understood and wanted to help him.

The loneliness and the fear started to leave him. He was no longer just Alan MacGregor, barely fourteen

144

years old, trying to fight off this big, aggressive High-bridge team alone. He was MacGregor, quarterback—one of eleven men all striving for the same purpose. He opened his mouth and started to call the numbers in a clear, cool voice, and then Hackett gave him the ball. As his fake to Bill Lee sucked in the Highbridge line-backers, he drifted away, still concealing the ball, fading toward the side lines with Sam Marvin cutting around behind him. He gave Highbridge a view of the ball then, when he faked his lateral to Marvin. Marvin held out his hands for the ball, and Alan stopped running.

The same Highbridge man was in on top of him again. He could see those intense blue eyes and the blood-streaked chin. Then he picked up George Pres-cott flashing across the field near the Highbridge twenty-yard line. As the Highbridge man was in the act of diving at him, Alan let the ball fly. He threw it calmly, cleanly, a perfect spiral down the field, and then he was thrown down violently. He never saw Prescott catch the ball, but the Westwood captain took it on the twenty, ripping off three more yards down the side lines before he was forced out of bounds.

The Highbridge player was breathing heavily as he got off Alan. He didn't say anything, but Alan saw the respect in his eyes and that did something for him. He was one of them now. He had stood up to them.

145

The clock was stopped when Prescott stepped out of bounds. As Alan trotted toward the huddle, he heard the noise from the Westwood cheering section. The Westwood players pounded his back in the huddle. They were grinning, still confident, even though they knew they had barely time for one more play.

Bill Lee said, "Good boy, Alan."

George Prescott opened his mouth to tell Alan the play, but Alan quietly said, "6-P." He was in command here; he was the field general calling the plays. George Prescott grinned at him, and they went up to the line of scrimmage.

Alan stood behind Pug Hackett. He even rubbed his hands the way he had seen Ronnie Hill do before putting them down for the ball. The Highbridge players were looking at him across the scrimmage line, and the worry in their eyes showed that they respected him. He stood there calmly, and he was a MacGregor, like his father and his uncle. He called his numbers—the same play, but to the opposite side of the field. He faked and faded and faked again, and there was George Prescott down on the goal line, streaking for the far corner.

Three big Highbridge men tore in at Alan, and he fired the ball between two of them before they buried him. He knew it was good, even before he threw the ball. Prescott leaped and caught the ball on the line. Two Highbridge men hit him, but he was into the end zone for the score and the game.

It was seven o'clock that night and the campus was quiet and deserted. Mr. MacGregor and his brother had stayed for supper and the big celebration in the dining room. The crowd was still inside; Alan could hear the singing as he walked across the grass with his father. The night was clear and cold and bright with stars, but there was no moon. Mr. MacGregor would be leaving in a half hour and he had suggested this little walk before going.

He said, "You might be first-string quarterback next year, Alan, or the year after."

"That's what I'll be fighting for," Alan said firmly.

"It was a great game," Mr. MacGregor said, "one of the greatest I've ever seen."

They were strolling under the trees now. Alan could hear the gentle rustle of dead leaves above him and the faint singing in the distance.

"It's a good school, Alan," his father said. Then he stopped and looked up. For the first time Alan realized that they had walked over toward the water tower and now were standing almost beside it. He, too, looked up

147

to the vast height above him and saw the tank clearly outlined against the starry sky.

Mr. MacGregor took off his topcoat and hung it over the branch of a tree. As Alan watched him in amazement, he said quietly, "Always had the feeling I'd like to go up there."

Then he stepped up on the concrete base, reached up for an iron rung, and started to climb the ladder. After he had gone up ten feet he stopped and looked at his son. Alan was watching him, as if hypnotized.

"Coming up, Alan?" his father asked.

Alan moistened his lips. Without a word, he mounted the concrete base and started to climb after his father. They went up steadily, never stopping, climbing up toward the stars, Mr. MacGregor a half-dozen rungs above his son. When they reached the platform which circled the round tank, they sat down, their legs dangling over the edge, and grasped the iron bars in front of them. They were both breathing hard from the climb.

Far below them and across the campus they could see the lights from the dining hall and the various dormitories. They could still hear the singing, but very faintly. Above them were the stars.

"It wasn't so bad, was it, Alan?" said his father.

148

They looked at each other in the dim light. Both were smiling.

"No, sir," Alan said. It would never be bad again. He knew that as surely as he knew that the stars above would never fall from the sky. It was a wonderful feeling.